SLEIGH BELLE

N.D. TESTA

N.D. TESTA
Sleigh
Belle

N.D. TESTA

Sleigh Belle

Trees
Frost Tree Lot

Sleigh Belle: 2024 Edition

This book was rewritten and republished in 2024 for a more thrilling reading experience. A former version was published in 2023

Artwork by: Ashley Testa

Edited by: Melissa Cole

Cover Design by: Emily's World of Design

Formatted by: Black Bow Publishing

Published by: Blue Eye Publishing House

ISBN E-BOOK: 979-8-9862189-3-9

ISBN PAPERBACK: 979-8-9862189-4-6

ISBN HARDCOVER: 979-8-9862189-5-3

Printed in the United States of America

CHAPTER 1

hat in the hot cocoa conundrum happened here?

Belle Winters' mind echoed with her grandma's favorite expression. She could hear the elderly woman's light-hearted raspy voice, and wondered what her grandma would think if she saw the barren estate that stood before her. Looking out the passenger window from her position in the driver seat, Belle wondered if she was at the wrong address.

"There is no way this is Frost Manor." Belle said as she gripped the steering wheel of her luxury SUV with one hand while checking the directions app on her phone with the other. She knew it had been years since she'd driven around town, but her memory wasn't that forgetful. Her phone told her that she was parked alongside Pine Cone Lane, and the monstrosity before her was Frost Manor. The faint clicks from the hazard lights were a tolling reminder of how much her life had changed in a week.

"I can't believe this," Belle exclaimed as she opened the car door. "It looks like this place hasn't been lived in for months. Where are the lights, the bells, the bows, the wreaths?"

Frost Manor was the crown jewel of Falls Village, Vermont. The European-style edifice was owned by the Frost family who had occupied the residence for the past hundred years. Each year,

1

they decorated the magnificent structure in the most elaborate display of Christmas cheer. It was a picturesque painting of holiday fantasy. People came from all over to admire the beauty of the elegant arches decked out in festive boughs of holly. Twinkling lights sparkled across the roof's edge and the stain-glass windows shimmered with seasonal cheer.

However, this was not the sight that met Belle's eyes.

The fifteen-bedroom mansion that once oozed elegance and glamor, was now a dilapidated state of Christmas past. The manor was in a condition of anti-holiday protest. An air of neglect lingered. Not a single wreath or light decorated its stone exterior. Nature had appeared to reclaim the property as bushes had over-taken the landscape, covering a portion of the windows. Ivy snaked up the chimney while weeds crawled up the walls. Walk-ways were covered in icy slush, the lawn was peppered with half-melted mounds of snow, and flecks of paint had peeled off the shutters. The overgrown trees with their bare skeletal branches made Belle feel like she was at a haunted house.

Belle hung her head. Sam would have never let this happen but he had died back in January. She remembered when she had flown in from New York City to attend his funeral then leave right after. That had been her life for the past decade: fly into town for less than twenty-four hours then depart. Now ten months later, here she was back in Falls Village with no schedule to keep, no rushing around, and no idea where her life was headed.

Belle shoved her hands in her pockets to try to chase away the cold. Her long hair blew freely around her head. *Mom said one of Sam's relatives had moved into the house. His grandson maybe? But there's no way any family of Sam's is occupying the residence with the house looking like this.*

Her boots clicked against the asphalt as she walked over to a set of iron gates that blocked the entrance to a long road that ran alongside Frost Manor. The path led to a part of the hundred acre property that was dedicated to growing Christmas trees. Families from miles around came in droves to find the perfect pine for their home. Before entering into the lots, there was a gathering area for pedestrians to get into the holiday spirit. In the center was a large handcrafted heirloom known as the Christmas Wishing Bell.

The bell was the reason for Belle's visit. In the past it had been tradition for people on their Christmas ventures to make a wish and ring the bell. Legend had it that if the wishers' hearts were pure and their souls full of compassion their dreams would come true. Many area residents testified to the bell's powers, including Belle, even though her past wishes had been little girl frivolous fantasies. Her childhood dreams had included getting a puppy, making the softball team, hoping her crush would ask her to prom, and attending an ivy league university. All those dreams had come to fruition, but sometimes she wondered if there had been a magical power in play or just her hard work paying off.

On this cold December day she wasn't looking for something tangible. Her wish was more abstract. She yearned to know where her life was headed and receive guidance on the right choice to make.

She pushed against the gate but it wouldn't budge. Looking down, she noticed a chain with a lock was wrapped around the bottom. Groaning, she pressed her forehead against the iron, letting the icy cold metal kiss her skin.

This is the worst month ever. It's bad enough I lost my job right before Christmas, now I can't even make a wish on the bell.

She raised her head. "Why are the gates closed? It's three weeks until Christmas. This place should be bustling with people. Why haven't they opened the lot or decorated the house?" She rattled the gate in frustration, then turned on her heel. In her slow trek through slush back to her SUV, a neon orange and black sign caught her attention. Stopping, Belle saw the words NO TRES-PASSING in all caps glaring at her. More signs followed, some nailed to the nearby trees and others positioned on the gates.

"What's going on?" Belle murmured. She got back into her car and started the engine. Moving the gear shift into drive, she steered the car a few feet forward into the driveway of Frost

Manor. While the gates to the tree lot had been locked tight, the gates to the estate were open. Belle pulled into the cobblestone driveway that formed a half-circle in front of the mansion. A Lamborghini SUV was parked in front of the five-car garage.

"Clearly someone lives here." Belle unfastened her seatbelt and opened the door to the chilly air.

Living the fast-paced city lifestyle for much of her life, Belle had adapted a mind-your- business mentality. However, being back in her country roots had her feeling a bit nosy or curious as her grandma used to call it. The frigid December air hit her in the face as she crossed the dreary landscape to the front door. She walked past a large fountain that featured a marble statue of a reindeer. The basin was filled with frozen murky water, and leaves protruded from the icy surface. Belle shook her head in disgust.

Approaching the entrance, a short octagonal sign near the front steps alerted her that the house was monitored by high security.

"What are they trying to protect against? No one would come near this place with a ten foot pole." Belle stepped onto the stoop and saw a doorbell camera next to the trim around the doorway. A press of the button garnered no response. After pressing it again, she wrapped her fingers around the lion-shaped door knocker and brought the handle down for three loud raps.

"Not even a wreath." Belle shook her head and glared disap- provingly at the bare door. She pulled her coat tighter around her slender frame.

No answer.

She pressed the button again. Maybe her half-frozen fingers hadn't gotten it right the first time.

Still no answer.

Maybe he isn't home.

Belle caught her reflection in the tempered glass of the door. Her brunette curls spilled past her shoulders and her brown eyes were filled with worry. Redness crept along her nose and cheeks as the frosty wind kissed her skin.

A crackling sound came from the intercom, jolting her out of her thoughts. A man's irritated voice echoed across the porch. "No solicitors allowed!"

"I'm not trying to sell you anything—"

"Can't you read?" the voice interrupted. "There are signs all over the place stating no visitors, no solicitors, and no trespassing. This is private property."

This is what you get for not minding your own business. Her inner thoughts chided her. Clearing her throat, Belle tried to stay calm. "I'm not trying to be a bother. I would like to speak to the owner about an important matter."

"I don't wish to be disturbed."

Belle rubbed her frigid fingers together. His angry response ignited an irate flame within her. "Why isn't Frost Manor decorated? My grandma and I were good friends with Sam Frost. He was family to us. He had this place decked out beautifully every year. When I was little, my grandma and I would help him tend his rose bushes." Past memories of happier times flooded her mind. "Then I went to college in New York to study art and for the past decade I've worked in the city. I was hoping the Christmas tree lots would be open so I could make a wish on the Wishing Bell." Her voice trailed off as she realized she had become lost in her own memories and was talking to a speaker.

"Lady, if I cared about your life, I would have asked. Who the hell do you think you are coming to my residence and giving me your life sob story? I don't care. Learn to read. No visitors!"

"Don't talk to me like that." Irritation pulsed in Belle's veins. "Where is the Wishing Bell?"

"The Wishing Bell is a legend full of false hope." His voice hissed as he mocked one of her favorite memories. "All it amounts to is a bunch of horrendous traffic bringing tourists to a town they've never heard of, to ring a bell and pray for some childish Christmas fantasy that will never come true. Look at you coming all this way to ask why I don't have a bell available for you to ring and make a stupid wish. Foolishness."

Words failed her. How could Sam have left this heartless man in charge of his most beloved possession?"

"Isn't it obvious? There isn't going to be a Christmas at Frost Manor. No one will be getting trees from the lot and nobody will be ringing that idiotic bell. I don't care if you knew my grandfather, I'm the owner of this house now. Leave before I call the police."

"Who are you?"

"Leave. You're on security footage. You're trespassing and disturbing my peace. Go and never come back. The authorities will be called next time. No Christmas at Frost Manor. Goodbye." His threat was emphasized with the crackling sound of the intercom shutting off.

Why did I even bother? Belle headed back to her car as a million thoughts rushed through her head. *Falls Village depends on Frost Manor for jobs, tourism, and Christmas joy. How could Sam have ever left Frost Manor in the hands of that embittered human?* For years, her routine consisted of breezing into Falls Village late on Christmas Eve and leaving early on the twenty-sixth. Now she was finally back in town for the whole holiday season and it wouldn't be the same.

Her phone dinged with a voicemail from the headhunting agency. Belle clicked the play icon.

"Hi Belle, it's Aubrey Bryson with Snowden's Recruiting Agency. I sent your resume to a couple of companies. I don't expect to hear back for a bit due to the approaching holiday. I know you're eager to start working again, but have patience. We will find you the perfect job. I'll call you if I hear anything."

Belle threw her phone onto the passenger seat. Of course it wouldn't be good news. Pressing the ignition, her car roared to life. She touched her foot to the gas, and the vehicle sped out of the driveway and down the street.

"Who does that beast think he is?" Belle fumed as she fumbled with the buttons on the radio. "He can't be Sam's grandson. No way." Sam had always been a kind, gentle soul with a neatly trimmed white beard and a dazzling smile. He had a plump frame and oozed Christmas spirit wherever he went. Two of Sam's favorite things were decorating the manor and his rose gardens.

Belle's mind drifted to the last time she saw Sam: Christmas Day last year. Their yearly visit had only been a few minutes on his porch while Belle waited for a taxi. She remembered he had asked why she never showed the art gallery her paintings. She had replied her work wasn't good enough to be in a museum.

Don't fear failure, Belle. Fear being in the same spot next year as you are right now. Those had been his last words to her as she placed her luggage into the back of the cab.

Emptiness gnawed at her soul and disappointment spread through her body. At this stage in her life, she should be reaping the benefits of her years of sacrifice. Now, she stepped into an unknown future and she had no idea what to do.

CHAPTER 2

"Belle, why on Earth would you go to Frost Manor?" Belle's mother asked as she piled stuffing on a plate and handed it to her. "This is my fault. I should have warned you about the changes. I was going to tell you tonight at our December-Giving feast." She brushed away a few stray locks of gray hair that had fallen into her blue eyes.

"You know I had to see the decorations. I wanted to make a wish on the Wishing Bell." Belle's stomach rumbled as she took the plate from her mom. She was happy that her family had gathered and cooked up a second Thanksgiving feast since she'd missed the real holiday due to a charity event at work. She stabbed the pile of mashed potatoes with her fork. It had been a waste of time attending the event. She had hoped that working over the holiday would have helped land her the vice-president position. Instead, she had gotten laid off a few days later due to budget cuts and low attendance at the gallery.

Her fork moved to the mound of stuffing and she pushed it around. Sacrifices were supposed to lead to joy, yet in her case, it had led to unemployment. Mountains of stuffed mushrooms, and macaroni and cheese were heaped on her plate. As much as she wanted to devour this delicious food, the altercation with the stranger at Frost Manor weighed heavily on her mind. After leaving the mansion, she'd gone straight home to her parents' farm. While it felt good to be back, she wasn't thrilled to not have her own place. After losing her job, she had given up her apartment to one of her friends and gone home to get her mental health right. Her mind drifted back to the voice from inside Frost Manor. In a small town that was full of so much joy how could someone be so miserable.

"Who was that man?" Belle asked.

"His name is Jake Frost," replied her father as he poured gravy over his turkey. "He's Sam's grandson."

"There's no way that man is related to Sam. He's nothing like him." Belle shook her head.

"Jake is more like Sam than you think," her father said with a chuckle. Deep wrinkles formed around his brown eyes.

"You're brave going over to the manor, Auntie Belle," her seventeen-year-old nephew Logan chimed in. "If I went over there, I would have thrown a rock through his window."

"Logan, don't talk like that. We don't resort to violence to solve our problems. That's vandalism and you'll get arrested," Belle's brother Grayson scolded.

"It doesn't matter. This Christmas is going to suck anyway." Logan shoved a forkful of corn bread into his mouth.

Grayson cast a look at his wife Luna who shook her head.

"Now, now, dear, don't say such horrible things. I know we are not fond of Jake but all the seasonal events that are held in Falls Village will continue as scheduled." Belle's godmother Violet Silk chimed in as she folded her napkin. "We are going to have the Christmas Market, the gingerbread house contest, and the snowman building competition."

Logan shrugged, "It doesn't matter. The Wishing Bell is what brings people to Falls Village. Now people will have to go two towns over to get their trees, and I won't get the seasonal job of netting the pines for customers."

Belle looked over at her nieces, whose angry expressions mirrored her nephew.

"Logan is right," agreed sixteen-year-old Aviva. "Everyone at school has been talking about making a wish on the bell. Now we can't make any wishes."

"Frost Manor is no more," said thirteen-year-old Ciella with a dramatic sigh. "What were you going to wish for Auntie Belle?"

"A new job." Belle stabbed her fork into the macaroni and cheese that was growing cold. "I don't understand. The Wishing Bell has been a part of our community for almost a century. Frost Manor too. Sam wanted it that way. Isn't there something the town can do?"

"Unfortunately, Frost Manor is private property. It's not a historical landmark," replied her father. "Jake is Sam's only living relative and he left everything to him. After the funeral, Jake moved into the manor. You had already returned to the city at that time. No one knows anything about him. He rarely leaves the house, he never comes into town, and he chases out anyone who tries to visit Frost Manor. Just before Thanksgiving, Mayor Janssens went to see him and asked if he was going to open the tree lot and the Wishing Bell. Jake told her that the Wishing Bell needs to be crushed and dumped into the ocean, and no more wishes will be made on his watch.

"He's a real beast of a man," added Violet, pushing her jeweled glasses up to the bridge of her nose.

"The whole town has nicknamed him the Beast of Frost Manor. Everyone at school was talking about it," chimed Ciella.

"He. Is. A. Beast." Violet punctuated each syllable for emphasis. "He has no care for anyone in this town. He just moved in and shut down what makes our town whole."

"Not to mention he has the entire place covered in surveillance like someone is going to rob him," grumbled Logan.

Belle's sister Josie waddled out of the kitchen carrying an apple pie. Steam rose from a lightly browned crust. "I can't even think about there not being a Christmas at Frost Manor. It makes me too emotional." She placed the dessert on the table and rubbed her stomach. "Why didn't Sam leave the manor to the town? We would've upheld his legacy."

"It was his place to leave to whomever he chose. Maybe he didn't know his grandson would do this," answered her husband Monty. "He seems to have money. I saw him leaving Frost Manor driving an expensive foreign car last week. Be careful dear, don't overwork yourself."

"I'm fine. Belle, I can't thank you enough for taking over for me at the bakery. The doctor said the baby will be here any day now." Josie looked down at her protruding belly.

"It's not a problem," replied Belle. "It'll keep me busy while I'm looking for another job. I put my resume into an agency to help me find work. Hopefully I'll hear from them soon."

"I wish you would just stay in Falls Village," sighed her mother as she put another biscuit on her plate.

"Mom, you know my life is in New York City now. I've worked hard to establish myself. I can't just leave it all behind." Belle folded her napkin and placed it next to her plate.

"Now that you're home, you can get back to work on your painting," her father said, changing the subject. "You still have your studio above the horse barn."

"I don't know, Dad. Maybe. You know I haven't painted in forever." Belle stood up.

"The talent is still there."

"Maybe the Beast will hire you to repair all of Frost Manor, Aunt Belle," joked Aviva.

"The guy is supposed to have a bunch of money, he has no excuse not to keep up the place and decorate it," Logan grumbled into his dessert. "He needs to be taught a lesson. He can't come into our town and take away one of our oldest traditions."

"I don't want to hear any talk of violence at my table, young man," Belle's mother said as she raised an eyebrow at her grandson.

"Don't pay him no mind, Grandma. He's just mad he can't use

the Wishing Bell to wish for the courage to ask Allegra Thomas on a date." Aviva laughed. Logan scowled and threw a piece of his turkey at her.

"Enough you two," snapped Grayson. "Finish your food and stop antagonizing each other."

Belle picked up her plate. "Josie, you said to be there at four in the morning?"

"Yes, I know it's very early but we have to start filling orders. Amelia will be there to help you and I'll be there after my doctor appointment."

Suppressing a grumble, Belle walked into the kitchen and turned on the faucet. She never had to wake up that early back in the city. The warm water flowed over her fingers and into the drain. Belle thought of her grandma and wished she was still alive. She had been very close to Sam. If only Sam had put it in his will that the Wishing Bell, tree lot, and decoration of Frost Manor had to happen every year. She picked up the cloth and scrubbed the plate.

"Belle," her father called. "I saw Joey Esposito at the hardware store yesterday. He said you still haven't gone to see him to get what Sam left you in his will."

His comment brought a collective groan from the family.

"Seriously, Belle?" Grayson cried. "It's been almost a year."

"I was busy." Belle dried her dish and put it in the cabinet.

"I can do that honey." Her mother entered the kitchen and took the dishcloth from her. "You had a long drive. Go rest."

"I don't understand how you haven't gone yet," chimed Josie. "I would be so curious to see what Sam left."

"Apparently Belle is the only other person beside Jake that was left something in Sam's will," added her father.

"Do you know what it is?" Josie turned to Belle.

"I have no idea. There wasn't an explanation in the letter that was sent to my apartment." Belle sat back down.

"Tomorrow make sure you stop by Joey's office after you're

done at the bakery," her father instructed. "Whatever Sam left you must have been very important."

"I think I'm going to head upstairs and rest." Belle replied. She gave her family a small smile and headed toward the stairs. A feeling of dread swam in the pit of her stomach as she climbed each step. Whatever Sam had left her, she hoped it wasn't in the mansion. After the altercation today, she had no desire to talk to or see the Beast of Frost Manor ever again.

CHAPTER 3

Belle leaned against the counter at her sister's bakery in downtown Falls Village. She stared into the lobby where there was finally a lull in the constant stream of customers. The inviting aroma of sweet and fruity notes filled the shop and enticed consumers for a taste of the popular desserts.

Wiping the sweat from her brow with her forearm, Belle glanced at the clock and saw it was around three thirty. She pulled her phone out of her apron. No messages appeared. Her mom had informed her this morning that her nieces and nephew would be coming to the bakery after school.

I wonder what's keeping them. I'll text them in a bit.

Belle shifted her weight from side to side as she gripped the counter. She wasn't used to being on her feet for so long.

"Belle, do we have enough pumpkin cheesecake and gingerbread cookies? Those are our best-selling items," her coworker Paola called from the kitchen.

Belle glanced at the display case. "We're good." The pies, pastries, and cookies enticed her but she'd already eaten enough. Belle grabbed a rag and wiped down the tables. As she looked around at the vibrant colors of the bakery, a sense of pride rushed through her. Her sister had done well for herself. After going to culinary school, Josie had opened Plum Kiss Desserts. Now it was one of the best sweet shops in the state. She was also an excellent wife and soon-to-be mother. Curiosity struck Belle as she wondered what it would be like to settle down in a small town. Even though she had grown up here, the fast-paced lifestyle of the city was all she knew as an adult.

Glancing out the large windows at the front of the shop, Belle could see all of the town's Christmas cheer. Street lamps were covered in garland and strings of lights. Wreaths hung from every door, and festive static clings were featured in every store window. Little shops up and down the street were decked out in their holiday best.

The cheerful atmosphere was interrupted by the loud 'ting-a-ling' of the bell signaling the arrival of a customer. Belle looked up to see Sheriff Falco entering the establishment. His eyebrows were furrowed and the downward turn of his mouth indicated that something was wrong.

"Good afternoon, Sheriff. What can I do for you?" Belle moved behind the counter, dropping the rag she had used in the bin and washing her hands.

"Where is your brother and his wife, Belle?" Sheriff Falco placed his arms on the counter and leaned against the glass.

"They're over in Pine Rock getting a Christmas tree and doing some shopping. The service there is spotty. They will be back this evening." Belle turned to face him. Falco had been the sheriff in the small town for as long as she could remember. He had watched her grow up along with her siblings.

"I was afraid of that. What about your parents?" The sheriff rubbed his graying temples.

"They are at an appointment. What's wrong?"

"I just got a call on the radio about a large group of teenagers trespassing at Frost Manor. Apparently the Beast called the cops. When the troopers showed up, the kids scattered, but your nieces and nephew were caught."

Belle's heart plummeted to her stomach. She couldn't imagine her nieces and nephew getting into trouble with the police, but after last night's conversation, she had her suspicions. "Are you sure it was them?"

"This is a small town, Belle, everyone knows everyone," the sheriff replied. "The Beast is throwing a fit and I need to talk to their parents asap."

A small smile twitched on Belle's lips. "You call him the Beast too?"

"The whole town does."

Belle laughed.

"You're not going to think it's funny when you find out the Beast is planning on pressing charges against your nieces and nephew," replied the sheriff.

Belle's smile disappeared. "What are you talking about?"

"He wants them charged with trespassing and vandalism."

"What? Why? They weren't the only ones who were over there," Belle exclaimed as she took off her apron and threw it on the counter.

"They were the only ones who got caught and they refuse to tell us the names of the other people involved."

"I'm coming with you. I'm their godmother and I don't want anyone else to worry." Belle walked to the kitchen door. "Paola. Amelia. I have to leave. It's an emergency."

After briefing her coworkers on what was going on, Belle grabbed her coat and walked in step with the sheriff. "Where are they now?"

"Over at Frost Manor. I told my deputies not to do anything until I got there."

Belle got into the passenger seat of the cruiser as Sheriff Falco turned on the ignition. The naked trees moved in a blur as the car left the center of town and drove down the ghostly road toward the mansion.

"I remember when this road used to be bustling with people on their way to the manor. Now look at it. Dead as a doornail." Sheriff Falco let out a low whistle.

Belle barely heard him. She felt jittery and her thoughts raced. What were her nieces and nephew thinking? They had always been good kids. Her stomach felt nauseous as she remembered Logan's words from last night about how the Beast needed to be taught a lesson. She shouldn't have stirred the pot with all the no Christmas talk.

"Why are they being charged with vandalism?" Belle turned to the sheriff. She needed to have all the facts before they reached the residence.

"Apparently the group of teenagers had it in their heads that they were going to destroy the manor." Falco glanced briefly at Belle and then back to the road. "I know, I can't believe it either. Any reason they would act that way?"

Belle rubbed the bridge of her nose. "I-I don't know. They were upset about the manor not being decorated for Christmas, the tree lot being closed, and the Wishing Bell. But I didn't think they would destroy a house over it."

"Let's not be rash. We'll wait until we get there before passing any judgment." Falco leaned his head against the back of the seat. "Off the record, no one in this town will blame these kids for doing what needed to be done. That Jake Frost is a pompous and arrogant fool with a ruthless temper. He gets gifted a prized estate and lets it rot away. Then he won't even carry on the tradition that helps bring in revenue for the town. Not to mention he's rude to everyone and doesn't bother to get to know the residents of the community his grandfather worked so hard to help. Fiddlesticks if you ask me."

As they rounded the bend, they were greeted with the sight of five police cars in the driveway of the manor. Some of the officers were chatting in a circle in front of the open entrance.

Falco pulled up alongside the other vehicles and Belle was out of the car before he could put it in park. She stopped in her tracks, clasping her hand to her chest as she took in the state of the mansion. Five of the lower windows were broken. Wrapping paper had been strung around the marble columns, bushes had been uprooted, tree branches were broken, and shattered ornaments littered the front yard. But the part that stood out the most was all of the spray paint. There was a giant X on the door and the word BEAST had been written in red paint all over the house. The reindeer fountain had been massacred with a collage of different paints and the cobblestones repeated the word 'beast' over and over. Then there were sayings written all over the garage and walls: "Frost Manor is for all of us," "Give us back Frost Manor," and "We need the Wishing Bell." Belle's stomach twisted in knots. How could her godchildren be capable of such violent acts?

"Where are the children?" asked Falco.

"They're inside, Sheriff," replied one of the officers. "With the Beast...I mean Mr. Frost."

Belle bounded up the steps and through the door. She stopped short as the old-fashioned beauty of the interior took her breath away. It had been so long since she had set foot inside this place that she had forgotten how stunning it was. A double staircase with wrought-iron designs and gold balusters greeted her. Above her was a vaulted ceiling trimmed in cream with a massive crystal chandelier that sparkled in the sunlight. Turning to her right, Belle hurried into the great room. The space featured cathedral-style ceilings and French doors that lead onto a patio. Logan, Aviva, and Ciella sat on the couch. Their arms were crossed and sullen expressions were plastered on their faces. A tall man stood in front of them with his back to Belle.

"Aunt Belle!" Ciella shouted as she jumped off the couch with Aviva. They threw their arms around Belle's waist. Logan followed them silently, his hands shoved into his pockets.

"Are you guys alright?" Belle asked. "What happened?"

"I'll tell you what happened. These children of yours have destroyed my house for no reason." The man snarled as he turned and faced them.

Belle's eyes widened as she struggled to keep the expression of shock from weaving across her face. The heir of Frost Manor was not the old and grumpy man she had envisioned him to be.

Instead, a handsome young man in his mid-thirties stood before her.

"Who are you?" she asked even though she knew the answer but couldn't believe it.

"I'm Jake Frost, the owner of this estate," growled the man. His green eyes studied her in pensive thought. "Wait a minute. I recognize that annoying voice. You're the crazy lady who came banging on my door yesterday. Now you bring your minions over here to vandalize my residence because I didn't decorate?"

"Excuse me!" Belle stepped forward. "First off, these are my nieces and nephew. Second of all, my voice is not annoying, and third, I'm sure there is a valid explanation for what has happened here. After all, my godchildren were not the only ones involved in this."

"Where is the sheriff?" mumbled Jake.

As if on cue, Falco entered the room. "What seems to be the trouble here, Mr. Frost?"

"I want these children arrested for vandalism and trespassing. I want this woman here charged with breach of peace and conspiracy." Jake pointed to Belle and the children.

"Belle? You want Belle arrested? Why?" Falco scratched his head. His expression concluded he thought Jake was crazy.

"Yesterday, she appeared on my doorstep, hollering about why I wasn't decorating Frost Manor and opening it to the public. Today her nieces and nephew trash my home. That isn't a coincidence." The muscles in Jake's arms flexed as he folded them across his chest.

"But they weren't the only ones who were involved," protested Belle.

Falco gestured for the adolescents to sit on the couch. "I've known you kids a long time. Tell me what happened."

"You think they're going to tell you the truth?" Jake snapped. "They're delinquents, liars, and criminals. They need to be in jail."

"Don't talk about them like that!" Belle cried.

"Mr. Frost, I'm going to need you to settle down so we can get to the bottom of this." Falco turned back to Logan. "What happened, son?"

"A bunch of kids from school were angry about Frost Manor being closed. Everyone decided to meet here after classes and send Mr. Frost a message that he can't do this to us. It isn't fair that he comes into our town and takes our traditions from us. I don't care if he's Sam's family or not."

"Whose idea was this?" asked Falco.

"Mine and two other people. One of the kids saw Mr. Frost leave the mansion early this morning. When we finished school, we checked and he still wasn't home. Then we sent out posts on social media telling all the kids to gather here. We were only going to spray paint a little, but we got carried away. Then someone threw rocks at the windows and broke them. The alarms started going off, the cops showed up, and everyone ran."

"Who were the other people involved?"

Logan didn't answer.

"You're not going to tell me who the other people are?" repeated Falco.

Logan remained quiet.

"There were around twenty-five of them," said Jake.

Falco looked at Ciella and Aviva who were also silent.

"Kids," cried Belle. "You need to speak up."

"No," replied Logan. "We aren't snitches."

"The only reason we got caught is because we couldn't find Ciella. It turns out she was by the Wishing Bell. By the time we found her and tried to run off, the cops appeared and stopped us," added Aviva. "Then he showed up too." She nodded at Jake.

"You may have been part of a group who caused the damages but you're the ones who got caught. I will ensure you are prosecuted to the fullest extent of the law. Some time in juvenile detention should stop you from leading a life of crime." Jake sneered as he raked his fingers through his curly hair and glared at them.

Belle's heart pounded. She turned to her godchildren. "Please tell us who was with you?"

The teenagers remained silent.

"I have cameras all over the place." Jake turned to the sheriff. "I'll send you the footage of the children vandalizing my home. However, it will be hard to identify them because many of them had their hoods up or their faces covered." He nodded at the scarves around their necks and the ski mask in Logan's hand.

"I'm sure we can come to some sort of resolution that doesn't involve something so extreme," Belle pleaded.

"Did you see how much damage has been done to my house? It's not only the outside that was severely damaged but the interior too. The rocks and chunks of asphalt that were thrown through the window damaged the walls and broke a few statues. Now the cold air coming into my house is making it feel like I live in Alaska." Jake gestured towards a large piece of rock that lay against a smashed wall.

"Mr. Frost, I understand you're upset. I'll call the construction company and have them board up the broken windows until you can get the glass replaced. Since the children won't tell who else was involved, I'll have to press charges against them. Come on kids, let's bring you downtown so I can book you."

"Sheriff. You can't do that. It'll be on their permanent records. Logan is about to start applying to colleges," Belle cried.

"What can I do, Belle? This is his property. He has them on camera destroying his house. It's criminal mischief -- that's a misdemeanor, you know that. They don't want to say who else was involved." Falco waved a few of his officers into the living room.

"What about a deal?" Belle blurted out.

"A deal?" Jake looked from the sheriff to Belle. "Are you talking about bribery? That's what you people do in this town? You try to bribe your way out of justice?"

"That's not what I'm saying." Belle paused to collect her thoughts. "I'm saying that I'll take care of the damages if you don't press charges against Logan, Aviva, Ciella, and the rest of the children involved."

Jake studied her. "How are you going to take care of the

damages? You don't look like the type who has the money to pay for repairs."

"I have money and I know people in this town who can get the job done right. I have always been good at art and interior design. I can get everything restored better than it was before." Belle glanced around the room. "After all, this place is in need of a facelift."

Jake turned away from her and stared at the shards of glass that littered the floor. "Will you make sure the children of this town stay away from the manor?"

"Absolutely," Belle promised. "I'll take care of everything, and I'll make sure the place looks good as new. I can even repair some of the other things that are worn."

"Aunt Belle, you can't do that," cried Ciella.

"We'll help Belle with the repairs," Logan told Jake. "It'll go faster that way."

"No. I just said I want all the children of this town away from my manor," Jake growled, whirling back around. "I've had about all I can take from you teenagers." He turned to Belle. "If you want to take on the children's debt, you'll do so yourself. You'll report to this place every day at eight in the morning and work on fixing the damages, then you'll leave at three in the afternoon. You will follow this routine until the job is done." Jake extended his hand to Belle. "Do we have a deal?'

Belle clasped her hand in his. "It's a deal."

CHAPTER 4

"I can't believe I just did that." Belle groaned as she placed her face in her hands. The smell of baked goods filled her nostrils as she sat at her sister's kitchen table. After the whole ordeal, she sought refuge in Josie's house as opposed to returning to her parents' home.

"I can't believe you made a deal with the Beast," Josie said as she took a tray of cookies out of the oven. She placed them on the cooling rack before taking a pumpkin cheesecake out of the fridge and placing it in front of Belle. She inhaled sharply as her hand went to her stomach. "Ugh, baby girl keeps kicking me."

"I don't know what I was thinking. I didn't want the kids to get in trouble. They're so young." Belle's body felt drained like she had run a marathon.

Josie plopped down next to Belle. "I don't know what to say. I have no idea what I would do if this little girl did something like that." She pulled the scrunchie out of her hair and shook out her blonde locks before twisting it into a new bun. "But I'm ready for her to arrive." She picked up the knife and sliced the cheesecake in equal portions. Grabbing the server, she put the pieces onto plates for Belle and herself.

The kitchen door burst open and Grayson stormed in. His coat was half-buttoned, his brown hair was uncombed, and his red scarf hung loosely around his neck. "Whoever said having children was a good idea, lied!" He slammed the door shut.

Josie held up a plate. "Pumpkin cheesecake?"

"Yes, please." He sat down next to them.

"Where's Luna?" Josie asked.

"Back at the house. There was so much tension that I had to escape. I told her I would be right back." Grayson replied as he shoved a forkful of pie in his mouth. "I-I just can't believe my kids did that. The Beast gave Sheriff Falco the security footage but he can't identify any of the other kids because their faces were covered. Jake said he won't press charges anymore because of your deal, Belle."

"Yes. Belle volunteered herself in servitude to the Beast to save the children's future." Josie narrowed her eyes at Belle.

"Why would you do that?" Grayson sighed. "We know nothing about this man, and you sell your soul to him. He could be a crazy person. He probably is crazy. You shouldn't have done it."

"It's not a big deal, Grayson." Belle assured him. She poked her fork into the cheesecake, leaving little holes in the orange filling. "I told him that I would take care of the damages to his house and help clean up."

"Belle, you don't have a job. How are you going to pay for that?" Grayson leaned closer to her. "I feel like you have an angle to this."

"I have savings and investments. Besides, it shouldn't take long to clean up the damage. And maybe I can convince Jake to decorate the manor for Christmas."

Grayson snorted. "I knew you had ulterior motives. Oh Belle, always the optimist. Good luck with that after the way he acted today. You'd have a better chance at seeing pigs fly."

"I hate leaving you high and dry at the bakery Josie. With this arrangement I won't be able to get there for work until after three."

Josie waved her hand. "Don't worry about it. Your nieces and nephew will take your place and work in the bakery as punishment for what happened today. Luna texted me. I'll have plenty of help."

"Luna might be angrier than me. She said they can't go out anywhere or hang out with any friends until Christmas and no television and no video games." Grayson shuddered.

"And the money that I would be paying them for working is going straight to you, Belle, to help cover the damages." Josie added.

"I can't accept that." Belle shook her head.

"Yes, you will." Grayson scraped his fork against his plate. "It's the least we can do after the heroic sacrifice you made for the children of Falls Village."

"Consider it paid time off," Josie added. "Oh!" She placed her hands on her stomach again. "These kicks are driving me crazy. Not to mention she's all curled up in my rib cage and I can't breathe."

"She'll come when you least expect it. Trust me, I've lived through it three times." Grayson stood up and took the empty plates. "I will do the dishes. You rest, sis."

"In other news, Joey stopped by the bakery and said you didn't go to his office, Belle," said Josie.

Belle groaned. "I was going to go and then the whole fiasco happened. I'll go tomorrow after I finish at Frost Manor."

"I wish Sam had left you the house," Grayson said as he began to wash the dishes.

"But he didn't. We asked Joey what Sam had left you since you were taking forever to claim it. But he said it was strictly confidential, and he was not allowed to reveal the items in question."

Once the dishes were cleaned and put away Grayson hugged his sisters goodbye. "I've got to get back home. Luna will have my head if I'm late. Good thing we live across the street." He hurried out the door.

"You go upstairs and rest. I'll stick around a little while longer. I'm not ready to go home yet," Belle told Josie.

Josie pressed a kiss to Belle's cheek before making her way slowly up the stairs.

Belle took a seat in front of the television next to a roaring fire. A Christmas movie was playing, but Belle left the sound off. She wasn't in a joyous mood. Instead, she got on her phone to look at job postings, and ended up making the mistake of mindlessly scrolling through social media. Seeing all the friends she went to high school with getting married, having children, celebrating job promotions, and different accomplishments in life made her heart weep.

At thirty-five years old, she thought she would be taking part in similar celebrations, but life had ripped the rug out right from under her. She felt as if she was starting from scratch, and she had no idea which way to turn.

She went into the photo app on her phone and pulled up a picture from her favorites section. It was a picture of her grandmother and Sam standing next to one of Sam's prized rose bushes. They had their arms around each other and were smiling for the camera.

Belle ran her fingers over their faces and a soft smile came to her lips. She wished she could talk to them right now. They always had good advice. She really wanted to ask Sam why he had chosen his grandson to take over the house. Surely he must have known how his grandson was. It didn't make sense. She knew Jake had never visited the manor while Sam was alive. If he had, she would have remembered him.

Closing the phone, Belle placed the device on the coffee table. She had enough emotional self-sabotage and pity for one night. The painting on the mantle caught her attention. It was a painting of the Wishing Bell. The silvery bell glittered in the glow of the twinkling Christmas lights. Belle got up and walked over to it. As she got closer, she recognized it was one of her own pieces. She had painted it for Josie as a gift twenty years ago. It has been ages since she picked up a brush.

Sitting back on the sofa, Belle rested her hand under her chin as questions simmered in her soul. Who exactly was this man that had vanquished all of the Christmas magic from Falls Village? Picking up her phone and opening the internet browser, Belle typed 'Jake Frost, Falls Village, VT' into the search engine. Nothing appeared. At least not anything relevant. She tried other ways to word the description but she didn't know where Jake had previously lived.

Belle leaned against the cushions feeling defeated. Ever since she had gotten unexpectedly laid off, it was as if a curse had woven its way into her life. Everything was a constant downward spiral of despair. Now she found herself involved with a beastly man who was sucking the town dry of all its seasonal joy.

CHAPTER 5

The sun's brilliant display of radiance over Falls Village couldn't take away the feeling of dread that loomed in the pit of Belle's stomach. She parked her car feet from the front door and stared at the barren entrance. If only her nieces and nephew had made better choices, then she wouldn't be stuck in this cold and lonely place. It had snowed last night but the dusting of fresh powder couldn't hide the air of misery that hung over the manor.

As Belle stepped out of the vehicle, the frigid air stung her lungs, and turned her breath into a blossoming vapor. Reaching across the seat, she grabbed a box of gingerbread cookies from her sister's bakery.

The five broken windows stood out like an eye sore. The plywood that covered the openings reminded her of a pirate with a patch. Her boots left a trail on the snow-covered cobblestones as she walked to the door. Removing her hand from the warmth of her coat, she pressed the bell.

No one answered.

"Here we go again," mumbled Belle. She took a deep breath and savored the quiet. It was the first time since returning to Falls Village that she had a moment of peace and wasn't caught up in the chaos. A memory from long ago surfaced in her mind of when she was a little girl standing in front of this entrance with her grandma. It had been her childhood dream that one day she would live in a beautiful home like this one with a man who loved her and children of her own. However, here she was, single and alone. Irritation flared through her and she pressed the button again. Then she banged the knocker three times.

"Why isn't he answering?" Moving forward to knock again, Belle was startled as the door opened and Jake appeared before her.

"You're late," Jake barked, glancing at the expensive watch on his wrist. "It's five after eight. You were supposed to be here at exactly eight o'clock."

"I was here at eight. You took forever to answer the door." Belle pushed past him and walked into the manor.

"It's a big house," grumbled Jake, following after her.

"A big anti-Christmas house," muttered Belle, turning on her heel to face him. She held the lavender box parallel to his nose. "This is for you."

"What's this?" Jake flared his nostrils and grimaced as if he found the little box utterly repulsive.

"Gingerbread cookies from my sister's bakery. I wanted to give them to you to apologize for the incident that took place yesterday," Belle explained.

"Great," Jake muttered sarcastically. "Another bribe." He took the box and placed it on the coffee table.

"What are you talking about?" Belle raised her eyebrows.

"You're trying to bribe me, aren't you? Well, it's not going to work. Just because you bring me cookies doesn't mean I'll forget our deal. You promised to fix the damages and help tidy up around here." Jake clasped his hands behind his back and walked over to the fireplace, distancing himself from Belle.

Belle rolled her eyes. "I'm not trying to bribe you. I figured you could use a little Christmas spirit since this place looks like a haunted house."

"Anytime anyone comes to a person's house with food or gifts, especially after the chaotic fiasco that occurred yesterday, it's textbook bribery. Let me guess. You're trying to poison me in retaliation for taking away your town's hopes and dreams of a Merry Christmas."

"You're insane." Belle's face grew hot at his ridiculous accusation. She walked over to him. "I would never do that. What kind of people do you think we are in Falls Village?"

"The kind of people who trespass onto property that isn't theirs and vandalize structures they claim to love." Jake whirled around and Belle collided into him.

With his face inches from hers, Belle felt the room around her melt away as her focus narrowed in on Jake's features for the first time. Well-sculpted brows framed his jade eyes that glistened with intelligence and secrets. A stray curl fell over his forehead, highlighting a few crinkles near the corner of his eyes. His strong jawline featured a faint stubble. High cheekbones and a straight nose drew attention to his full lips. Years of dedication to fitness were evident in his lean, muscular build. A flush crept over Belle's face as the flames in the fire crackled behind them. Her chest fluttered like butterflies were trapped in her rib cage. Jake was a captivating work of art and she wanted to take in every detail. Her heightened sensation was followed by repulse as she remembered this was the man who was demolishing her childhood memories. How could someone so mesmerizing be so beastly?

"Maybe if you explained your reasoning for shutting down Frost Manor, everyone would understand. Your grandfather would have never wanted it this way." Belle stammered as she ran her tongue over her slightly chapped lips.

"Enough." Jake snarled and pulled back from her. "I'm so sick of hearing about what my grandfather did. I'm not him."

"Oh, we can see that."

"Take this." Jake shoved a piece of paper into Belle's hands.

"What's this?" Belle looked at the note.

"It's the list of everything you need to do today as part of our agreement."

Belle raised her eyebrows. Who did this Beast think he was? "I said I was going to help pay for the damages. I'm not your servant."

"I never said you were. But you did say you would help tidy up the place. I spent the whole summer in Europe. There are many things I wanted to get done around here, but I never had the time. Now you can do it for me."

"I—" Belle stuttered.

"Unless you want me to have your nieces and nephew arrested and charged with vandalism and trespassing," Jake sneered.

Belle glared at him.

"Tomorrow I'll have another list for you. You'll come here Monday through Friday. The weekends you can have to yourself."

"How generous you are." Belle resisted the urge to roll her eyes.

Jake turned to go down the hall. "I'll be in my study working. You have free rein of the house. You can go anywhere you like except for the room at the end of the west hall. Don't go in there." Jake looked over his shoulder at her and narrowed his eyes. "I put the shovel in the closet by the front door. You'll need it. And please hurry, I can't stand the sight of the graffiti any longer." Then he vanished behind the door of his study.

Belle crumpled the note into a ball. "What a beast." Then she unfolded it again to see the first task: *shovel the driveway and walkways*. "He's rich and he can't hire someone to do this?" Grabbing the snow shovel out of the closet, she threw open the front door. The driveway and sidewalks seemed to go on forever.

"What did I get myself into?"

CHAPTER 6

The ornately carved cuckoo clock chimed as Belle walked into Joey Esposito's law office around four in the afternoon. She was frozen to the bone, tired, and hungry. While shoveling the driveway, Belle had made calls to a number of graffiti removal companies. She hoped to have someone scheduled to come out to the manor within the week. After that her next tasks included polishing silverware and dusting paintings. All day Jake remained in his office. When it was time for her to leave, she yelled goodbye but he didn't answer. Belle didn't want to know what would be in store for her tomorrow.

Joey's firm was down the street from the bakery. It was an end space next to a gift shop. The location was small, with a waiting room and Joey's office in the back. Belle flexed her achy, callused hands as she entered and saw Joey at his desk, staring intently at his laptop. His dark hair was peppered with gray, and the creases near his eyes gave him a distinguished look.

Only a few years older than her, Belle had dated Joey in high school. He had always planned on staying in Falls Village to practice law, whereas Belle had wanted to see the world. Many years later, Joey had found happiness with a wife and three children.

"Belle." Joey looked up from his desk and stood up. "Come in.

It's about time you paid me a visit. I thought I would have to send Sheriff Falco to escort you to my office." He chuckled and gestured for her to sit down.

"Hi Joey." Belle settled herself into one of the plush chairs in front of the large oak desk. Her throbbing body thanked her as this was the first time she had sat down all day.

"Give me a minute. I have to get the paperwork." Joey walked over to a tall filing cabinet and rummaged through the drawers. Behind the desk were built-in bookshelves that were filled with leather law books. On the walls were Joey's diplomas, along with pictures of his wife and kids. His wife was pretty, and all three of his kids looked like miniature versions of him.

"Ah, here we go." Joey took out a thick file and placed it on the desk. He pulled out a sheet of paper, his gray eyes scanning it. Then he handed it to Belle. "In case you weren't aware, in Sam's will he left everything to his grandson Jake, with the exception of one item." Joey walked over to a wall safe and punched in the code. He pulled down on the lever and the door opened. He removed a small box wrapped in gold paper and adorned with a red bow. "Sam wanted you to have this."

"What is it?" Belle stared down at the gift Joey placed in her hands.

"I'm not sure. Sam never told me." He sat back down in his chair, his eyes fixated on the mystery item. "Open it and find out."

With a tug on the ribbon, the bow slipped off. Belle ripped off the paper and opened the lid. On a red satin pillow rested a small ornament. Belle wrapped her fingers around the delicate silk string and held it up to the light. The intricately carved ornament was a bronze bell. Along the top of the bell were paintings of poinsettia leaves. Along the bottom were drawings of holly. The middle of the bell bore a still image of a horse and sleigh in front of a mansion.

A gasp escaped Belle's lips as she recognized the design. "This is a replica of the Wishing Bell. It's beautiful." She moved the trinket between her fingers so it caught the light and sparkled. "Did Sam say what the meaning was behind this gift?"

"There is no explanation or letter." Joey leaned back in his chair and stretched his arms over his head. "He told me the explanation would come with time."

"Sam was always good with riddles," Belle replied. She moved her wrist back and forth, expecting to hear the ring of the bell, but the only sound that met her ears was silence. "That's strange," she murmured. Turning over the bell, she saw that the clapper had been removed. "Where's the clapper?"

"The what?" Joey asked.

"The clapper is the piece of the bell that makes it ring. It's not there." Belle explained. She shook the bell hard again to demonstrate.

"I don't know. The box was sealed when Sam left it with me. I don't think it's been tampered with. Maybe he didn't want the bell to have a clapper." Joey shrugged.

"But that's what makes the beauty of the bells; it's the melody they sing."

"My guess is Sam is up to his usual tricks. But I need you to sign here to confirm I've given you your inheritance." Joey slid a piece of paper across to her.

Belle picked up the pen and signed her name. As she walked out of the law office and into the Christmas-covered streets Sam's gift nagged at her.

A bell with no clapper. Belle had a feeling this had been done intentionally. Was she the one who was supposed to find the missing clapper and make the bell sing again?

CHAPTER 7

I *hate being on hold.* The sound of jazz music blared out of Belle's phone as she leaned against the kitchen counter at Frost Manor. She had been waiting ten minutes for a representative from a graffiti removal company in Birch Lake. *Why isn't someone answering the phone? There can't be that many people that need graffiti removed.*

Lost in her thoughts, Belle picked up the ornament Sam had given her. Since she had received Sam's gift, the silent bell plagued her thoughts. She twirled the object between her fingers to distract herself from lashing out at Jake. The Beast of Frost Manor was taking advantage of the predicament and using her to save on hiring a cleaning company. She couldn't even begin to imagine how much a company would charge to do the job she had taken on for free. It would take a miracle to bring this monstrosity back to its former glory.

Suddenly, the saxophone's low, drawn-out melody was replaced by the sound of a woman's voice. The receptionist told Belle they would send an estimator to the manor on Friday to assess the damages. This was taking longer than Belle had anticipated.

I wish these companies would hurry up and do the job so I can be rid of Jake for good.

She opened the calendar app on her phone. Donato Ricci had told her he would come out within the week to fix the damaged windows and walls. He owned one of the best construction companies in town and was a friend of her family.

Belle turned her attention back to the kitchen. She was currently in the process of taking everything out of the cabinets and wiping the insides. However, the immense task couldn't distract Belle from the question she'd been asking herself for the last few days: *Why would Sam leave me a replica of the Wishing Bell with no clapper?*

Deciding she needed a break, Belle put on her coat and walked out the back door. Fresh air filled her lungs, helping her focus her thoughts. With her hands snuggled in her pockets, she walked across the yard, past the barns, and down the dirt path that led to the entrance of the Christmas tree lot.

At this time of year, Belle would usually see the vacant lot to her right full of cars. People would enter through the arbor of poinsettias and holly, and grab a shiny saw from the rack. After trudging through the snow and finding the perfect pine, families would pull their freshly cut Christmas trees on sleds, laughing and singing carols as they walked. The scents of hot chocolate and gingerbread wafted through the air, and a fire pit enticed people to sit and warm their bones. On their way out, visitors would choose an evergreen wreath for their front door. Her feelings of nostalgia were washed away by the empty space that surrounded her. A boarded-up hut sat abandoned and empty. Rust had taken over the blades on the saws and the arbor that marked the entrance to the Christmas trees stood as empty as Belle felt.

The one thing that had stood the test of time was The Wishing Bell. In its usual spot next to the fire pit, the heirloom rested in the shadows of Christmas past. The antique was three feet tall and hung from a yoke of American Elm wood. Carved into the wood was a saying Belle knew by heart.

Making a wish is casting a spell from the heart to allow miracles to take place.

The bell had been handcrafted by Edmund Frost, Sam's great uncle. The bell had initially been cast in brass, but one would never know with the beautiful paintings that covered the heirloom from the crown to the lip. The top of the bell had poinsettias painted around it while holly covered the lower part of it. In the center was a beautiful replica of Frost Manor with a sleigh passing in front, while the other side featured fields of pine trees.

The saying on the bell was the one Sam had repeated to her and her friends when they were children. He advised them that with a little faith and belief, anything was possible, and Christmas was the season for wishes to come true.

Belle pulled the mini ornament from her pocket and held it in her palms. The sunlight made the decorations on the brass sparkle. A sudden thought came to her mind. There had to be a reason Sam had given her a replica. Could the Wishing Bell be silent too? Belle crouched down to look inside the bell. Her hunch was correct as she discovered the Wishing Bell lacked a clapper. Placing her hand on the bell, she pushed forward. The massive treasure moved back and forth, but no sound came from within.

First the ornament, and now the Wishing Bell. Two silent bells. That wasn't a coincidence.

"Where is the clapper?" Belle looked inside the bell again. This time, something caught her eye. Near the top was an envelope taped to where the clapper should be. She leaned forward to pull it down and opened the thick paper to reveal a note written in fancy script.

A silent bell
tolls the pain of a broken heart

Its clapper gone
Like the sense of identity
When betrayal hits home
However, when surrounded in melancholy darkness
a pinch of hope
can shed light
and spread warmth
when the soul has become ice

The elegant loops and swirls written in black ink jumped out to her. She would recognize Sam's handwriting anywhere. This is why no explanation had been given. He had gifted her the ornament with a missing clapper knowing that curiosity would get the better of her. Sam wanted her to find the clapper, and this poem had to be a clue.

But why all the mystery? Why wouldn't he just tell me?

Belle glanced up at Frost Manor. Jake might know where the clapper was. After all, Sam was his grandfather. But Jake didn't seem like the kind of person who would be excited about a Christmas scavenger hunt.

If Sam wanted Jake to find the clapper, he would have left him an ornament too. But he didn't. That means he wants me to do it myself.

Sam always had a twinkle in his steel blue eyes and a reason for why he did certain things. Belle shoved the ornament back into her coat pocket. She would have to trust his judgment and find the answer to the questions herself. However, she didn't have a clue where to begin.

CHAPTER 8

I'm sick of working in a haunted house every day.* Belle thought as she wandered the halls of the manor the following morning. A yawn escaped her lips. She had spent a sleepless night reading and rereading the note Sam had left for her. But she still hadn't cracked the meaning of the cryptic message. Placing her hands on her hips, Belle looked down the drab hallway. Only a few weeks until Christmas and Frost Manor couldn't be more in protest of the holiday season. Former memories of happier times at the mansion filled Belle's head and she became lost in her own thoughts. She needed to save this place if it was the last thing she did.

"That's it. I can't take it anymore. I'm doing all this tidying, I should be able to decorate this house and make it festive. After all, I'm working for free for who knows how long." She placed her hands on her hips. "I know Sam has a bunch of Christmas decorations in storage somewhere." Her feet took her down an unfamiliar corridor with a set of oak doors at the end of the hall. Images of reindeer engraved in the wood brought a smile to her lips. Sam always loved Christmas, unlike his Grinch of a grandson.

Hmm. I don't remember this room. Maybe the Christmas decorations are in here.

She wrapped her hands around the brass handles and opened the doors. Her eyes widened as she stepped into a solarium.

The room had escaped the curse of ugliness that ran rampant throughout the manor. It was a massive octagon that featured glass walls and a dome ceiling. Sunlight bathed in through the panes. Lush greenery enhanced the botanical paradise. Vines wove along the rafters, and parlor palms were positioned along the walls. Potted plants of various shapes and sizes lined the floor and window sills, creating an indoor jungle oasis. Hanging baskets overflowed with ferns and trailing ivy. However, what stood out the most to her were the roses that filled the solarium. Red, pink, purple, orange, yellow, and white blossomed from the trimmed bushes.

In the center of the room was a sofa and two armchairs with a coffee table in between them. On the top of the table was a stack of gardening books and historical novels. It was the most well-kept room in the entire mansion. Despite the cold temperatures outside, the space was warm thanks to the giant heaters placed throughout the room.

Belle turned in a slow circle to marvel at the beauty. It was at that moment a shadow caught her eye. Belle stopped and saw on the coffee table, a glass vase that held a single black rose. She sat down on the sofa and brushed the petals with her fingertips. *Black roses are not natural. What is the significance? Could it symbolize a love that has died or a broken heart?* Belle paused. This had nothing to do with Sam. He had been married for a long time. Even though he was devastated when he lost his wife almost thirty years ago, Belle had never seen a black rose anywhere on his property. Her thoughts drifted, she had lost her grandfather the same year as Sam's wife. She remembered how Sam and her grandma had bonded over their lost loved ones and eventually formed a life-long friendship. This rose must have something to do with Jake. Belle stared at the black rose. Could there be a connection between heartbreak and a missing clapper?

"What are you doing in here?" a beastly voice roared behind her.

Belle jumped to her feet as the door slammed and Jake stood in the center of the room. His face was irate and a massive scowl crossed his mouth.

"I..."

"Didn't I tell you not to enter the room at the end of the west hall?" he demanded.

"I'm not in the west hall." Belle replied.

"Yes, you are. This is the room at the end of the west hall." Jake stepped closer to her. "I told you that you could go anywhere in the manor your heart desired and you insist on going into the one room I said was off-limits. Don't you know directions? I thought you said you knew this place like the back of your hand. What's wrong with you?" Jake threw up his hands.

"Why do you have to yell like a wild beast? It was a mistake. It's been a while since I've been here and there are so many rooms in this mansion, I can't keep track." Belle snapped and placed her hands on her hips.

"This is a sacred space," Jake retorted, "and you don't have any respect."

"What do you mean I don't have any respect? If anyone isn't showing respect right now it's you. I said I was sorry and I told you it was a mistake. I was just looking for Christmas directions and went down the wrong hallway. It's not a big deal."

"Christmas decorations? Again with this festive nonsense," Jake snarled.

"This place looks like a ghost lives here." All the anger Belle had been feeling about her past, present, and future erupted like a volcano. "I don't understand your problem. All you do is yell. Can't you talk like a normal human being? You deserve the nickname everyone in this town calls you. You're a beast. A miserable, ruth-less beast. I'm here to fix damages, not to be your personal maid. You let this house go to waste. All this work should have been done when you first moved in. Christmas only comes once a year, and you'd think you would keep up your grandfather's traditions so everyone in the town would like you instead of hate you." Belle threw up her hands. "And what's so intrusive about me seeing a room full of roses? This place is a work of art; it shouldn't be hidden away. These roses are gorgeous. They are better than the ones my grandma and I used to help Sam maintain."

Jake's chest heaved as he took in a deep breath. "For the last time, you're not the owner of Frost Manor, I am. I'm sick of you coming into my domain with your sugar plum fairy thoughts and holiday spirit. If I don't want to decorate, I shouldn't have to. This is my house." He pointed to the door. "Get out. Just get out!"

"You really are a beast." Belle shook her head. "I'm done with this. I've tried to work with you and you're just nasty. I don't know how you're even related to Sam. He was the nicest person in the world. But you? You're a monster."

She reached into her pocket and took out the ornament. Walking up to Jake, Belle grabbed his wrist and slapped Sam's last gift into his palm. "Here. Maybe this will remind you of the Christmas spirit that your grandfather had. I'll still pay for the damages, but I'm done helping with this house. I quit."

CHAPTER 9

The nerve of that man. Belle slammed the solarium doors shut with all her might. The bang rattled the walls of the old house. Veins throbbed in her temples as she stormed down the hall to the front door. White-hot rage coursed through her as she slipped her balled fists through her coat and wrapped her scarf around her neck. Snatching her keys from the kitchen counter, she opened the front door and hurried down the steps. Just as she reached her car, the chirp of a cardinal made her look back at Frost Manor one more time.

The barren front yard, boarded-up windows, and red graffiti begged her not to leave. Sadness crept into her soul like water over fire. Frost Manor needed her. Maybe she shouldn't have been so harsh with Jake. He did have a point. As much as she hated to admit it, this was his house and his rules. He didn't have to go on with tradition and decorate the house if he didn't want to.

Belle kicked a small pile of snow that had formed on the driveway. She should apologize to Jake for her behavior but the Beast probably needed time to cool down. The mystery of the Wishing Bell still nagged at her. She would go look at the heirloom again then return to the manor and talk to Jake.

Her boots crunched on the snow as she crossed the front yard and walked down the dirt path to the Christmas tree lot entrance. Cold stung her nostrils, and her warm breath created white puffs in front of her. She reached into her pocket and took out the note she had taken from the bell.

> *A silent bell*
> *tolls the pain of a broken heart*
> *Its clapper gone*
> *Like the sense of identity*
> *When betrayal hits home*
> *However, when surrounded in melancholy darkness*
> *a pinch of hope*
> *can shed light*
> *and spread warmth*
> *when the soul has become ice*

"What are you trying to tell me Sam?" whispered Belle as she reached the Wishing Bell. She reached into her pocket for the ornament only to find it empty. Pangs of guilt seared through her heart. She should have never left the bell with Jake.

"A silent bell, well, that's definitely the Wishing Bell." Belle walked around the structure again. What if this was all a waste of her time? Maybe the letter didn't mean anything at all. But if that was the case, why had it been taped inside the bell?

Greenery caught her attention and she stared at the arbored entrance to the Christmas tree lots. It had been years since she had entered those fields. A brisk walk in the cold air was exactly what she needed to clear her head. Stuffing the note into her pocket, she strolled under the arbor and felt as if she had stepped through a portal into the echoes of Yuletide past. Wooden signs displayed arrows that pointed to the various fields where Fraser Firs, Norway Spruces, Scotch Pines, and Blue Spruces resided. The crisp air carried the earthy scent of pine needles. Rows upon rows of various heights and widths of evergreens stretched before her.

But it was the eerie silence that sent chills down Belle's spine. The farm looked like a ghost town. There were no crowds of people on the hunt for their Christmas tree, no couples holding hands among the pines, and no laughter from children. The joy was gone.

A rustle in the trees beside her caught her attention, making her realize she'd wandered deep into the lot, out of sight of the main entrance.

"Hello?" Belle tensed and looked around. Out of the corner of her eye she saw what appeared to be the tail of a dog disappear among the trees. The chatter of squirrels cackled above her head as they rustled about in the barren branches. Her eyes followed the direction where the dog had gone. Curiosity got the better of her, and she stepped over a fallen log into the woods, leaving the tree fields behind.

Belle had never seen this part of the farm. Mazes of trees and paths weaved their way deeper and deeper into the property. The snow was higher here than in the farmed tree lots, and Belle had to pick her knees up to make her way along the trail. She wasn't sure where she was going, but being out in nature gave her a sense of peace and clarity.

I shouldn't have spoken to Jake that way. I don't know anything about him. I shouldn't follow the judgment of the town. Who knows what he has been through?

Belle stepped out of the woods into a clearing. Her eyes fell on a frozen pond. Trees surrounded the body of water. The snow and icicles on the branches glistened in the afternoon sunlight. Benches were scattered around the area.

What a beautiful spot. This must have been a place for people to ice skate years ago.

She moved to the edge of the pond. A glazed reflection of her wind-chapped face stared back at her in the ice. Her puffer jacket hung on her slender frame. A wet slap of melting snow from the trees above her landed on her neck and shoulders, leaving glistening drops across her scarf. As Belle removed her scarf to shake out the damp particles, a gust of wind ripped the scarf from her fingers and sent it for a ride to the center of the glassy lake.

"Seriously?" she groaned.

Belle tapped her foot on the surface to test the ice. There were no cracking sounds, but she picked up a rock and threw it onto the pond just to be sure. It bounced along the ice and stopped near the center without any issues. Normally, Belle wouldn't walk onto icy ponds when she was alone. But this scarf had been made for her by her grandma and she couldn't bear to lose it.

Belle placed one foot on the ice, pushing down a little harder than usual. *I'll just move across the ice as fast as I can and get back.*

Steadying herself, Belle walked lightly on her toes across the frozen pond. She paused every few feet and listened for cracking but was met with silence.

It didn't take her long to reach the spot where her scarf lay delicately on top of the mirrored surface. She bent down, picked up her grandmother's gift, and slung it around her neck. She was about to breathe a sigh of relief when she took a step, and the wrenching sound of ice shattering met her ears.

Coldness ripped through her as her entire body was submerged under water. A gasp escaped her blue-tinted lips as her head broke through the surface. The frigid temperature took hold of her. Her body felt like tiny needles were pricking her skin. She felt hot mixed with cold then a numbing feeling. Her rapid heartbeat pounded in her ears as panic flowed through her. She kicked her feet in a desperate attempt to keep afloat. She moved closer to the edge of the watery hole she was in and tried to pull herself back onto the ice, but it broke under her weight. Her strength was fading and her clothes felt heavy. Her head grew foggy as she made one last attempt to pull herself out of the icy trap. To her dismay, she slid back into the water with legs like an anvil. The weight threatened to drag her to a watery grave. Through the fogginess in her brain, she heard what sounded like the rumble of an engine.

She thought she heard yelling and a dog barking. Everything was becoming a blur. She couldn't feel her feet or her legs, and she had no idea if she was even maintaining the kicks that had been keeping her above the surface.

"Belle!" she heard a voice call, but she couldn't process who it was. Her brain felt dizzy.

A rope slapped down on the ice in front of her. A loop was attached to the end.

"Put it around yourself!" The voice commanded.

With the last few ounces of strength she had left, Belle slipped the loop over her head and arms, getting it down to her waist. It tightened instantly and she lurched forward, out of the water and onto a thicker section of ice. Her body was limp as she was dragged across the frozen pond. She was relieved to not hear anymore cracking. The world seemed to dim around her as her vision faded, the rest of her body going as numb as her legs.

The last thing she was aware of was a strong arm encircling her and the warmth of another person against her body. A dog barked by her side.

I'm alive, thought Belle as she gave a silent thanks for the stranger's help.

Before she could see who her savior was, darkness took hold.

CHAPTER 10

Crackle! Snap! Sizzle!

The popping and hissing of flames engulfing dry wood greeted Belle as the world came into focus bit by bit. A groan escaped her lips. Disorientation clung to her like cobwebs in a forgotten corner. Her head throbbed, spreading a dull ache through her skull with each breath. Her eyelashes fluttered open, revealing wood beams running across an unfamiliar ceiling. Her body still felt like ice and protested every movement, but a sliver of warmth was starting to make its way through her limbs. As her sense of self began to return, questions swirled in her mind. She tried to recall the moments after her rescue but her memory offered only fleeting glimpses.

Where am I?

Taking in her surroundings, she saw she was lying in a king-sized bed with a blanket over her. Moving her frozen fingers to her side, Belle realized her wet clothes had been removed. She was clothed in a robe. Laying against the plump pillows, her eyes traveled the room. In front of her was a huge stone fireplace with a roaring fire in the hearth and a large television fastened above the mantle. Giant sliding glass doors led out to a balcony. The room was decorated sparingly which made it feel empty despite its massive size.

Am I in Frost Manor? She turned her head, and saw a figure seated in a leather chair next to her. He was looking at something on his phone, but there was no mistaking the curly hair and muscular stature.

Jake?

As if sensing her eyes on him, he raised his head and looked at her face.

"You're awake." He put the device on the armrest and rose to his feet. The typical harsh and unwelcoming expression had been replaced with one of concern as he moved to her bedside.

"What happened?" Belle struggled to a seated position as pain flowed freely through her. Jake leaned over and adjusted the pillow behind her back. Then he sat on the edge of the bed a few feet from her.

"You fell into the pond and almost drowned." He replied.

Belle remembered the strong arms that surrounded her when she had been freed from the ice. "You rescued me?"

"Yes."

"How did you know where I was?" Belle pulled the covers closer to her waist.

"Every inch of this property is under surveillance, even in the wooded parts. It's all monitored from my office and phone. After our argument in the solarium, I was shocked to see your car still parked in the driveway. I went to the cameras and saw you entering the tree lot. Then I grabbed my snowmobile and decided to follow you. I thought I lost you when Jingle found me and led me to where you were." Jake explained.

"Jingle?"

As if on cue, Belle heard a panting sound. A brown and white Saint Bernard entered the bedroom. His large and powerful body lumbered across the wood floor. The canine laid his massive head on the mattress next to her, begging to be pet. An avid dog lover herself, Belle gave the Saint Bernard a friendly scratch behind his floppy ears.

"This is Jingle." A rare smile spread across Jake's lips. "He was my grandfather's dog. He bought him about a month before he passed. Jingle has been trained to rescue people trapped in the snow. He brought me to you and I saw you had fallen into the water. On my snowmobile, I have a motorized pull chain attached to the back. I was able to use the rope to pull you from the pond. I called the paramedics as I drove you back to the house. They got here fast. They helped me get you into the room, then they removed your clothes and put my robe on you to keep you warm. They checked all of your vitals and determined that you had not been in the water that long, so there was no need to go to the hospital. You just needed a few hours to get your body back to normal temperature."

"How did you know what to do?" she asked.

"I was in the army for twelve years until I was thirty. Then I was honorably discharged after getting injured." Jake scratched Jingle behind the ears. "I was worried you were badly hurt, Belle. I'm glad you're alright. What were you doing going out on the ice like that?"

"I wasn't planning on it. The wind took my scarf and blew it onto the pond. It was a gift from my grandmother, I had to get it. I thought the ice would hold my weight." Belle replied as she looked down at her hands. "I'm sorry, Jake. I really didn't know that was the forbidden room. I shouldn't have kept bothering you about decorating the manor. You're right. This is your house and you can do whatever you want."

Jake leaned forward and covered her hand with his. His surprise gesture silenced anything else she was going to say. The scent of his cologne wafted to her nostrils, a mix of sandalwood and rosemary.

"I'm sorry, Belle. This time of year isn't the best for me and I've had a lot on my mind. I shouldn't have taken it out on you. You're right, the solarium is a room full of beautiful roses and it shouldn't be hidden away. It's just that Christmas time brings a lot of sadness for me. Every year I hope the holiday will pass quickly and quietly so I can get back to my normal routine."

Guilt gripped Belle's chest. She hadn't taken the time to consider the reason why Jake didn't want to decorate the manor. There had to be a very painful reason to make him not want to follow his grandfather's traditions.

Silence stretched between them as they stared at each other. Belle could feel the heat radiating from his body and she couldn't tear her gaze from his sculpted lips. Her heart rate increased and she felt the last bit of cold melt away. A sudden desire to lean forward into Jake gripped her.

What am I doing? I shouldn't be feeling this way. He's still a beast after all.

Jake broke the silence with the clearing of his throat. He turned his head and got up from the bed. Walking over to the dresser, he grabbed the first of two plastic bags that were positioned next to a stack of clothes. Her clothes.

"I put your phone in rice once I realized it was wet. The other bag has all the items that were in your pockets. There are your keys and something that looks like a letter but I'm afraid the water may have damaged it. I washed your clothes and dried them while you were resting."

Belle was speechless. This was the first time she had seen the side of Jake that wasn't beastly and she wondered if she still was dreaming.

"Thank you. I appreciate it." Belle looked around the enormous space. "What room is this? The guest room?"

"No. It's my room." Jake put the bag down and walked to the door. "The guest rooms in the house are all in the process of being renovated. This was the only room that had a bed." He paused. "One of the paramedics that revived you knows your family. I told him to call your parents and let them know what happened. They should be on their way to come get you. You shouldn't be driving home in your condition. When you're ready you can get dressed."

Jake called to Jingle who let out a woof and followed him. The door closed leaving Belle in the room by herself.

It took her a moment to process everything. She couldn't get over the fact she had been sleeping in Jake's bed. The Beast of Frost Manor's bed and she was wearing his robe. She inhaled deeply, breathing in his scent that lingered on the fabric. Then she looked to the left and right at the large amount of space that stretched before her in the king size bed. Jake had rested his head on this pillow and his body had laid on these sheets. The covers that surrounded her had kept him warm at night. Belle didn't know if she should be intrigued or uncomfortable. Many people wouldn't loan their bed to a complete stranger.

Belle threw off the covers and was grateful her legs had regained their power. She slid off the bed and walked across the floor plagued by a little stiffness. Leaving Jake's robe on the chair, she put on her clothes. She was happy to feel the warm fabric rub against her skin. The troublesome scarf sat on top of the bureau. Belle placed it over her head and smelled the fresh scent of lavender laundry detergent. Then she grabbed the plastic bags.

"Belle?" A muffled voice called to her.

Wrapping her fingers around the doorknob, she peered out into the quiet hallway. Jake was nowhere to be found.

"Belle!" The voice was clearer now. It sounded like her mother.

Belle made her way toward the immaculate double staircase. Standing at the top, she looked down to see her mother, Josie, and Grayson entering through the front door.

Josie glanced up and an expression of relief crossed her face. "There she is."

Belle was greeted by a plethora of hugs as she reached the bottom of the stairs.

"Oh honey, I'm so glad you're ok. Chase Miller called me and told me how you fell in a frozen pond at Frost Manor," her mother cried.

Belle nodded as her family continued to talk.

"You gave us such a scare! I thought I was going to go into labor!" Josie added, rubbing her stomach.

"Come on, honey, let's get you home. Grayson will drive your car and we'll go in mine." Her mother said as she took Belle's arm and led her to the front door.

Belle paused, a strange thought crossing her mind. "Who let you in?"

"No one," Josie answered. "The door was wide open when we arrived. We thought the place was empty until we saw you."

From the corner of Belle's eye, she could have sworn she saw a shadow moving along the wall on the floor above them. Her head turned sharply, expecting to see someone there, but the silhouette had disappeared.

CHAPTER 11

The first whisper of dawn crept around the edges of the curtains, spilling light into Belle's childhood bedroom. Warm rays covered her face in a soft golden glow as a rooster crowed outside. Belle opened her eyes and stretched her arms over her head. After her episode in the lake yesterday, exhaustion washed over her. She had no desire to move. Pulling the covers tighter around her, Belle tried to warm away the cold, achy feeling in her bones.

She glanced around the room. Many pieces of her artwork were displayed on the walls, and the small bed she rested on made her feel like she was a child again. Never in a million years did she think she would find herself living in her old bedroom. It was like she had gone backward instead of forward.

I need to get my own place.

Her memory drifted to the interaction with Jake. Her heart fluttered when she remembered how he had covered her hand with his. His eyes had been full of concern at her predicament. She couldn't believe he had come looking for her even though she had been pushy and prying into his personal business. His manner had thrown her for a loop. The Beast who had been angry and yelling in the solarium had turned into a kind, considerate, apologetic man. Belle thought back to how Jake had left the door open for her family, but didn't show his face when they arrived. He had chosen to remain secretive and aloof.

He is capable of being decent, yet he still chooses to act like a beast.

Belle shifted in the little bed. Her mom and the doctor had told her to take the next few days off but she felt restless. The get-up-and-go hustle of city life still ran through her blood. The rice bag containing her phone caught her attention as it lay on the dresser. Sliding off the bed, she put on her robe and removed the device from the rice.

I hope this works. I can't afford another phone right now.

Settling back into bed, Belle held her breath as she pressed the side button. Relief washed through her as the screen lit up. Turning her attention to her nightstand, she noticed the other plastic bag with a piece of paper inside.

Sam's note.

Leaning over, Belle took out the note, fearing the worst. The paper had become fragile and damp. With tender fingers, she opened it. To her dismay, a water stain blurred the cursive calligraphy. Belle reached down and placed the paper near the heater.

Her apprehension turned to solace as Belle remembered she had taken a picture of the writing with her phone. Laying her aching body against the pillows, she pulled up the photo app and found the picture of the riddle. Copying the words, she pasted them into the search engine to see what would appear. The only results were a few random poems that had pulled keywords from the note.

Sighing, Belle threw her phone next to her. The device bounced a few times on the mattress before settling down. A knock sounded at the door. Belle lifted her head to see Josie's concerned face peering into the room.

"How are you feeling?"

Belle gave her a small smile. "The real question is, how are *you* feeling?"

"I'm ready for all of this to be over and for baby girl to be here."

Josie replied as she opened the door the rest of the way and sat down at the edge of Belle's bed. "But I'm not the one who fell in a frozen pond yesterday."

"I'm surviving. I feel like there is an ache deep inside of me that I can't shake," Belle groaned.

"I know that feeling. It's probably the lingering effects of almost having hypothermia." Josie's attention moved to the note drying on the heater. "What's that?"

"It's a riddle I found at Frost Manor," Belle answered. "One that I can't seem to solve."

Josie raised her eyebrows. "Oh, really."

Belle poured out the whole story to her sister, from Sam's last gift to the note in the Wishing Bell. Maybe her sister could offer some advice to help her solve the mystery.

Josie took Belle's phone and read the note. "This is quite poetic. But what does it mean?"

"I don't know," Belle sighed. "That's what I've been trying to figure out."

"Maybe it is a clue that leads to a hidden fortune Sam has left you." Josie reached forward and grabbed Belle's wrist. "Maybe you'll be rich."

"I doubt that. Everything on that property belongs to Jake."

"Maybe it'll be a magic Christmas spell that will give Jake a change of heart. We all know that beastly man hates holidays with a passion," joked Josie.

"He really isn't that bad once you get to know him. Something in his past is causing him to hate Christmas. I just wish I knew what happened." Belle ran her fingers through her messy hair.

Josie stood up. "He sounds more like Dr. Jekyll and Mr. Hyde mixed with the Beast. Now you need to get some rest and I need to go down to the bakery and check on all of the children."

"Children?"

"Sheriff Falco couldn't identify the other kids in the video because their faces were covered and no one would talk, so he decided to teach all of them a lesson. He went to the school and talked with the administration. They are requiring that all the children perform community service. Today hundreds of teenagers are going to volunteer at the different establishments in town. Now I have more help than ever before. I need to get going. Mom made soup for you when you're ready to eat." Her sister paused at the door, her gaze drifting across years of paintings hung on the old farmhouse walls. "I do love all of these paintings you made, Belle. You should really get back into your art."

As her sister closed the door, nostalgia resurfaced in Belle's mind. When she was younger, she had been an avid painter. Throughout her teenage years, she had created many paintings that she had given to others as holiday and birthday gifts.

I can't believe I painted all of these. It feels like another lifetime.

A sinking feeling settled in the pit of her stomach; it had been so long since she had picked up a paintbrush. Part of her missed it and another part didn't want to remember the pain that came with her talent. She got out of bed and stared at her artwork. There was a painting of their house, one of the barn, and a few of the animals. However, it was the one by the window that caught her attention.

It was an artistic design of one of the windows at her home during Christmas. Burgundy curtains were pulled back revealing the twelve panes and a little mound of snow on the sill. Positioned in the window were candles. Wax dripped down the sticks as yellow light glowed on the wicks. Sprigs of evergreen wove their way around the candles. Belle turned her head from the painting and looked at the window in her room. The candles glowing on the sill were battery-operated, and not the real ones she remembered. Belle looked back at the portrait and ran her hands along the base where she knew her signature and the date would be. "I was a freshman in college when I painted this."

'A pinch of hope can shed light and spread warmth.' A candle can shed light, and it's warm. Could Sam have been referring to a candle?

Sam always had lots of different candles decorating his house. Of all the Christmas decorations he brought out each year, candles were his favorites. But which candle could he be talking about?

The thought plagued her as she headed downstairs. Reaching the bottom of the steps, she was greeted by the family's golden retriever, Jolly.

"Hey girl," she murmured, rubbing Jolly's neck and behind her ears. Jolly's tail wagged back and forth. Her luscious gold coat shimmered in the Christmas lights and her pink tongue hung out of her mouth.

Bursts of laughter rang from the living room as Belle entered. Her mother sat on the couch in front of a cracking fire, visiting with her godmother, Violet. Their heads were bent over a thick photo album that covered their laps. Chuckling, they pointed at the various photos. Her mother looked up when she heard Belle enter the room.

"How are you feeling, honey?" Removing the album, her mother rose to full height and hugged her. "Come join us."

"I'm feeling better," Belle replied as she sank into the armchair next to the couch.

"Thank the Lord you're alive." Violet exclaimed, clasping her chest. "I'm grateful the Beast was there to rescue you."

Belle gave her a small smile. She hadn't told anyone how Jake had given up his bed and robe to allow her to recover. "What are you doing?" She leaned closer to the couch.

"We're taking a trip down memory lane. Your godmother found this old album in her attic. It has decades of pictures from the Christmas Gala," replied her mother.

"Gala?"

"That was long before you were born." Violet said. Her eyes held a faraway look of happier times. "For years on December twenty-third, Falls Village used to host a ball to support charities for families in need. Everyone would get dressed up fancy and have a night out. There would be music and dancing. It was a grand time." Violet rose from her seat and stretched her arms out wide in a dramatic stance. She twirled around as if she was dancing the night away. "I miss those days."

"Why did it stop?" Belle tightened the sash on her robe.

"We used to hold it at the community center, but the place burned down almost forty years ago. The building was old, and the town didn't have the money to rebuild it. A developer bought it and turned it into a grocery store." Her mom closed the photo album.

"You could have held it in another location?"

"There are no other places in Falls Village that would accommodate that many people. Ah, well, at least we have the memories." Her mother placed the large collection of photographs on the coffee table. "Go eat. There's hot soup on the stove. Your body needs to regain its strength." She paused. "I heard you finally visited Joey and got your inheritance from Sam. What was it?"

"An ornament of a silent bell." Gloom spread over Belle when she realized the piece was still in Jake's possession. Taking a deep breath, she explained everything that happened. She needed all the help she could get.

Violet adjusted her shawl. "I wonder what Sam's point is in all of this?"

"Oh, you know Sam. He always enjoyed a good mystery. It was his way of teaching lessons or meddling when he shouldn't. I wonder which candle he's referring to. Frost Manor had so many of them," stated her mother.

Belle's stomach grumbled. "I don't know. I'll be in the kitchen if anyone needs me."

The aroma of chicken noodle soup felt like a comforting embrace as she entered the kitchen. She lifted the steam-covered lid of the pot to reveal a bubbling broth. Belle ladled a portion into a bowl and sat down at the table. She thought about how Jake didn't want anything to do with Christmas. However, if she wanted to solve Sam's riddle, she needed to figure out where the decorations were. The location they were stored in had to contain the specific candle Sam was speaking of. Belle raised the spoon to her lips and let the warm broth slide down her throat. The heat soothed her soul, the noodles were soft, and the vegetables flavorful. When she returned to Frost Manor, she would try to locate the decorations herself. She didn't want to cause Jake any more anxiety, but her work to solve the mystery wasn't done yet.

CHAPTER 12

It took another day before Belle felt like herself. The following morning, she stood in front of the still-barren front door of Frost Manor. The beating of her heart seemed to amplify with each passing second. She didn't know what she would say when she saw Jake. Even though they had made amends, she hadn't been able to shake the feeling she felt when he looked at her. To her surprise, the entrance opened immediately and she found herself face-to-face with the man himself.

"Belle. I didn't expect to see you so soon. I didn't check the cameras. I thought you were the delivery man," Jake stated. His sweatpants were slung low on his hips and his thermal top was tight around his chest and shoulders.

Clearing her throat, Belle looked down at her boots to clear her mind. "I promised to help fix the damages and get this place tidied up. I intend to keep my promise." She slipped past Jake and walked into the foyer. "The window people are coming today to repair the glass and I'm still in the process of hiring a graffiti removal company." Turning around, she handed a platter to Jake.

"More cookies?" Jake raised an eyebrow as he took the plate. His green eyes glanced at the array of treats under the plastic covering.

"I made them." Belle walked closer to Jake and pointed at each cookie. "These are gingerbread cookies and sugar cookies. Over here are my favorites, thumbprint cookies and snickerdoodles. I wanted to thank you for saving my life, and I'm sorry for being so intrusive in your domain." She glanced up at him and he held her gaze, sending goosebumps along her skin. "Anyway, the repair people should be here around nine." Taking off her coat, Belle hung it on the coat rack.

"That's in fifteen minutes." Jake headed toward the kitchen and placed the platter on the center counter. "I'm going to have to reschedule my meeting. I need to make sure everything is done right." He tapped his hands nervously against his thighs. "I think I left my phone in my office."He turned around and headed in the opposite direction. Belle followed him.

"I was planning on staying and overseeing everything, since I was the one who called them in the first place," Belle continued.

"It's fine, I got it," Jake called over his shoulder. "Why don't you go feed the animals? That can be one of your tasks for today."

"Frost manor has animals?" Belle asked.

"Of course. Sam loved animals," Jake replied, pausing outside the office door. "His animals have been here for the past decade. When I inherited the manor I didn't have the heart to sell them." He turned to face her. "I thought you said you knew Sam well?"

Jake's words stung and Belle hung her head. "I don't remember. Like I told you earlier, when I was little I came here all the time with my grandma. Then I went to college and got a job in the city. My visits here mostly consisted of a twenty-minute chat on the porch during the holidays."

Jake nodded and opened the office door, strolling inside.

"I had forgotten so much about this place. I feel like I'm seeing it for the first time with fresh eyes. I wish I had visited more..." Belle's voice trailed off as she stepped through the door frame.

The office was a sanctuary of dark wood. Two large windows framed with heavy velvet curtains overlooked the backyard. Built-in bookcases lined the walls, their shelves bursting with thick leather-bound volumes. A large fireplace adorned with intricate carvings sat against the far wall. A massive oak desk against the opposite wall sported two computer monitors, and behind the leather chair were five massive televisions hooked onto the wall. The screens had been separated into different sections. Belle not only saw views of the interior of Frost Manor, but she also caught glimpses of the barns, the Christmas tree lot, the pond, and the forests. She could even see the animals in their stalls. Jake hadn't been lying when he said every inch of this property was covered in surveillance.

Jake walked behind his desk that was cluttered with papers, pens, and envelopes. He rustled through a stack. Glancing up, he observed Belle's wide-eyed expression. "I wasn't joking when I said I had heavy security."

"But why?"

"I guess that's a habit of being part of the army for so long. One can never be too careful. This is a multi-million-dollar estate. It needs protection," replied Jake.

Belle was about to respond when something on the opposite wall drew her attention. It was a painting of Frost Manor at Christmas time.

"Where did you get that?" She took a step toward the portrait.

Jake pulled his phone out from under a mountain of folders. "Oh, that? I'm not sure. It's been in that spot for years. This used to be grandpa's office. I haven't changed anything except for adding the surveillance monitors. I wondered where he bought that painting. It's stunning."

"I-I painted it," Belle replied quietly.

"You're a painter?" Jake asked, his eyebrows raised.

"A long time ago. I made that picture for Sam for his birthday. I was sixteen. I can't believe it's still there," Belle exclaimed.

"I assume you paint for a living then?"

"No, I..." Belle was saved from admitting she was unemployed by loud beeping sounds coming from outside. On the monitors she saw the contractor trucks in the driveway. "The repairmen are here." She breezed out of the office and toward the front door.

Opening the door revealed two vehicles parked in the driveway. One of the men had already hopped out of the truck and slammed the door shut.

"Donato." Belle opened her arms to her former classmate as she walked down the steps.

"*Buongiorno*, Bella." A muscular Italian man with dark hair and a dimpled smile wrapped her up in a tight hug. "I couldn't believe it when my father told me you had called him to repair the damages on Frost Manor." He looked over at the exterior and shook his head. "*Mamma Mia,* I admire your bravery to fix the destruction, but you shouldn't have done it."

Belle sighed and looked at the manor. "I know, Donato. But I couldn't let Jake throw my nieces and nephew in jail."

"You shouldn't have to pay for this. Let that *stunad* pay for his own windows. He has his own money. He doesn't even need the Frost fortune. He has millions. You shouldn't have to spend your vacation here."

Belle shifted her weight; Donato didn't know she was unemployed either. "A deal is a deal."

Donato flicked his hand forward from under his chin in disgust. "Like I said, the Beast can use his own money, especially since he took this beautiful estate from our town. My father and I are already in agreement that we aren't going to charge you. Your family has done so much for us throughout the years. This guy might be a beast, but we aren't. In my opinion, he can just stay with the broken windows and walls. He's not honoring his grandfather's legacy at all. But since you insist on working with him, I'll volunteer my services as well."

Belle was about to protest but she knew there was no arguing with Donato when his mind was made up. "How long will it take to change the windows?"

"We should be able to fix everything today. We have enough

men on the job. But this is a very old house. Hopefully we don't run into any issues."

"Thank you for doing this. I'll be in the barn if you need me. I think Jake will be making an appearance shortly," replied Belle.

"I look forward to his presence," mumbled Donato as he took a toolbox from his cab.

Belle strolled around the side of the manor and headed toward the barns. Barking followed her. It was Jingle bounding over the snow-covered grass. He circled around her, his tail wagging.

"Hi Jingle." Belle leaned down and stroked the Saint Bernard's head. She walked over to the first barn and slid open the door. Inside was a bunch of farm equipment.

No animals here. They must be in one of the other barns.

Trudging back across the yard, Belle tried the second barn. The door creaked open revealing a massive interior. Earthy scents and a musty aroma of hay, old wood, and animals filled her nose. The sprawling space had been sectioned into different stalls holding cows, pigs, sheep, and horses. Naked beams hung overhead and sunlight filtered through the cracks in the weathered walls. The rhythmic sounds of animals filled her ears. She peered into the various stalls and found the animals freshly cleaned and well stocked with hay and food.

Belle looked down at Jingle who stood panting next to her. "Why would Jake tell me to feed the animals if he already did?"

The Saint Bernard turned in a circle and barked.

Belle decided to hang out in the barn, instead of returning to the house. She took her sweet time visiting the animals and playing with them. After she had finished, she took a walk. From where she stood, she could see the front yard of the house. Donato and his crew were in the process of replacing the windows while Jake stood nearby watching the action. A black puffer vest hugged his chest and his jeans conformed to his body perfectly. Jingle ran out of the barn and loped along through the snow to Jake's side. He reached down and scratched the dog behind the ears.

Stop staring at him. Focus on the task. This is the perfect time to search for the candle Sam was referring to. Belle snuck up the back steps and bounded into the house. Her eyes landed on a candle placed on the table next to the front door. Clasping her hands around the glass holder, she was perplexed to find the candle was Christmas tree scented. She hadn't expected that especially since Jake despised the holiday. She turned the jar upside down and looked for a note or description. There was nothing.

Taking off the lid, Belle brought the waxy center to her nose. The piney scent filled her lungs. Replacing the top, Belle ventured off to look for more candles in the house. Making her way through the first floor, Belle grabbed every one she could find and was disappointed not to find a clue.

Warm Apple Pie, Vanilla, November Rain, Sage...

"What are you doing?"

Belle flinched and almost dropped the jar. Jake stood in the doorframe. His arms were folded and his jaw clenched.

"I-I was just seeing what needed to be tidied up."

Jake's mouth twitched. "You know I have cameras all over the place. I can see everything from my phone. Now would you care to explain to me why you are going from room to room, picking up candles and looking underneath them?"

"I was trying to find something," Belle replied.

"I could tell. But underneath a candle?" Jake raised his eyebrows.

"I didn't want to upset you," Belle continued.

"What do you mean?"

"It has to do with Christmas," finished Belle.

Jake flinched at the word but nodded. "Go ahead, Belle. It's fine. Tell me."

Belle's shoulders slumped. "To be honest, I don't know what I'm looking for. You remember the ornament I gave you the other day? Your grandfather left it to me in his will. The tiny bell doesn't have a clapper. It's an exact replica of the Wishing Bell. I did some investigating and I found a note hidden inside the actual bell. The Wishing Bell outside doesn't have a clapper either. The letter was a riddle and I think it's telling me I need to find a candle."

Jake paused and reached into his pocket. "You mean this ornament you gave me the other day?" He pulled out the miniature item.

"Yes." Belle took her phone and showed him a picture of the note.

Jake looked over her shoulder. "That's my grandfather's handwriting."

"Do you know what candle Sam could be talking about? Maybe you can help me." Belle's hopes were dashed when she saw the look on his face.

Turning away from her, Jake shook his head. "I don't understand. What is with this town and its Christmas cheer? I can't seem to get away from it."

"But there has to be a reason why this note was placed there," Belle insisted.

"That's just like my grandfather. He was a dreamer and a romantic. He always believed that Christmas and the magic of love went hand-in-hand. When people had problems in their lives, he always wanted to help, but sometimes there are things in life that can't be fixed. You're wasting your time. My grandfather always talked in riddles. All this talk of the holiday makes me sick," Jake groaned.

"You do know you have a Christmas tree scented candle by your front door, right?" Proclaimed Belle.

"I didn't put that there. A week before the town's children vandalized my home, I hired an interior designer to come and spruce up the place. On her first day, she came intent on decorating this place for Christmas, so I fired her. That scented candle must have escaped my gaze, but it's going in the garbage. I will be so happy when this holiday is over." Jake threw up his hands.

Belle remembered how he had said that Christmas was a time of pain and she didn't want to upset him. "Jake. It's fine. I'll figure out the mystery of the Wishing Bell myself. Our town loves

Christmas because it's a time to celebrate and give thanks for all our blessings. It's a time of love, hope, and joy. We decorate to spread cheer and goodwill. That's why Sam always decorated the manor and opened the Christmas tree lot. He wanted people to be able to get together with their loved ones and make memories. Your family created the Wishing Bell to help make people's dreams come true and feel happy during the holiday."

"The Wishing Bell is stupid. It's just a gimmick to give people hope when there is none. You sound like something out of a TV commercial," snarled Jake.

Belle stiffened. She couldn't imagine what horror Jake must have gone through to make him talk this way about Christmas. "I'm sorry I brought it up. I'll get back to doing my job."

As Belle exited the room, she heard the crash of the Christmas-scented candle hitting the floor. Jake had gone back into beast mode. A feeling of pity swept through her and she wished there was some way to help him be happy again.

CHAPTER 13

After leaving Jake in his beastly mood, Belle returned to the barn. She sat on a bale of hay in the sheep pen, enjoying the company of the white fluffy animals. Their curious faces licked her hands searching for treats. Belle patted their wooly bodies. Christmas was approaching, and the thought of going into the new year jobless weighed heavily on her mind. One of the sheep rested its head on Belle's lap, and she scratched behind its ears.

At this point, I wish I was a sheep. Then I wouldn't have to worry about finding a new job or money. I could just lay around, eat hay, and enjoy life. She kicked at a stray piece of bedding. Life wasn't fair. One minute she was living her dream, and then the next she was starting over at the bottom. Leaning her head against the barn wall, Belle tried to let the gentle *baaing* of the sheep calm her. It was then she thought of Sam's riddle.

It has to be a candle. But what kind of candle? Why couldn't Sam just be specific? Why all the secrecy?

Her thoughts drifted to Jake. She was beginning to think of him as Dr. Jekyll and Mr. Hyde. He had been so nice to her when she had gotten injured and was cordial this morning, but as soon as she mentioned Christmas, he became unhinged. She scolded herself. She should have known by now not to bring up the topic of Christmas. He may be a beast, but Jake had feelings like the rest of the people in town.

"Belle."

Raising her head, Belle saw Jake standing in the aisle of the barn. Getting up from the hay bale, she stepped out of the sheep pen to meet him.

"I'm sorry. I shouldn't have snapped at you like that." He looked down at his boots.

"I'm sorry. I shouldn't have brought up the subject. I didn't mean to upset you."

"I was the one who told you to tell me." Jake reached into his pocket and took out a shiny object. Gently, he pressed the ornament into her palm. "You're far more deserving of this trinket than I am. My grandfather was a hopeless romantic, but he was a good judge of character. I know there's a reason he left the bell and the note for you."

Belle closed her gloved hand around the gift, and put it in her pocket. "Thank you. I just don't understand why he didn't explain what it meant."

"Grandpa loved puzzles and mysteries. He always wanted to take people on a journey." Jake took a deep breath. "I'll help you figure out the riddles."

A smile spread across Belle's face. "Thank you, Jake."

"Grandpa also had a way of getting into people's heads. I was thinking about the riddle, and if he is referring to Christmas then we'll have to look through the Christmas decorations." There was a hint of bitterness in Jake's response.

Belle wanted to ask why he hated Christmas, but she knew this wasn't the right time. Instead, she remained quiet as they walked out of the barn.

"I'm pretty sure the candles are in the storage room in the garage. The one that's not attached to the house. I remember my grandma had this beautiful vintage candle she would put on the front sill. Maybe that's the one grandpa is referring to. I need to go check on the repairmen. You can start and I'll join you."

Belle nodded, heading toward the garages. A five-car garage was attached to Frost Manor. Feet from it was another four-car garage that stood by itself. A loud creak announced her arrival as Belle opened the side door of the four-car garage. The immense space was painted white. Three expensive cars were parked inside, along with a few motorcycles, a quad, and two snowmobiles. Cabinets framed the walls. At the far end was a skinny door with holly boughs painted in each corner.

That must be the storage room.

As Belle walked toward the door, she paused to look at the exotic cars with uniquely crafted frames, shiny paint, and tinted glass. Opening the storage room door, she found a decent-sized space brimming with yuletide decor. Shelves upon shelves were filled with boxes labeled garland, wreaths, lights, ornaments, and more. Belle turned in a slow circle, taking in all of the decorations. A box on the lower level caught her eye, and she squatted down to take a closer look. The word 'candles' was scrawled across it in sharpie along with the word 'fragile.'

This might be it.

With delicate hands, Belle lifted the box off the shelf and placed it on the workbench in the center of the room. Removing the lid revealed a mound of candles wrapped in thick green and red tissue paper. One by one, Belle took each of the items out and unwrapped them. A collage of red, green, and gold covered the bench. Some candles were shaped like pine cones, others were snowflakes. There were different sizes, shapes, colors, and scents but none of them gave any indication they were the answer to Sam's riddle.

"How's it going?" Jake entered the storage room with Jingle at his heels. A disgusted look crossed his face as he glanced around at the boxes of Christmas cheer.

"Not good. There are so many candles," replied Belle.

"There are a lot of rooms in the manor. When grandpa decorated, he always went all out."

"None of these have a note." Belle sighed.

"It's got to be here somewhere," Jake said. "Let me try." He reached into the box and grabbed one of the tissue-covered candles. After unwrapping it, he shook his head and placed it next to the others.

They continued to search through the boxes in silence. Belle felt antsy. She wished she could understand Sam's purpose for sending her on this wild goose chase. The silence made her uncomfortable but she didn't want to talk about Christmas. Instead, she decided to focus on general conversation.

"I know your grandfather left you the manor, but what made you want to move here to Falls Village?" She asked.

"I decided it was time for a change," Jake replied as he rummaged through another box. "Have you lived in Falls Village your whole life?"

"Pretty much. I lived here until I went to college. Then I got a job in the city and only came to visit on holidays." Belle turned another candle upside down to check the bottom for a note.

"City life. Nothing quite like it." Jake removed a red paper covering and let out a whistle. "This is it." He placed the candle onto the workbench. It was medium-sized, encased in a glass holder. An old-fashioned Christmas tree was painted on it. Patches of snow and ornaments decorated the branches and there was a small candle on each bow. A vintage Santa stood in front of the tree, holding a basket of apples. He had one of the fruits in his hand, and he was feeding it to a baby reindeer that stood next to him. The craftsmanship and attention to detail was immaculate.

"This is exquisite," whispered Belle as she leaned in for a closer look.

"I remember seeing this candle shining bright from my grandparents' window sill every Christmas." Jake slid his hand along the bottom and pulled out a small index card. The fancy script glistened in the overhead lights as he handed the note to Belle.

Glancing down at the cursive calligraphy, Belle groaned. "It's another riddle."

"You thought my grandfather was going to tell you his purpose after one clue?" Jake chuckled as he leaned on the counter. "He probably has a whole bunch of clues for us to find. This is a treasure hunt. He used to do this all the time when we were kids. What does this one say?"

Belle cleared her throat and read the riddle.

Dashing through life
can leave one unfulfilled
Forgetting to stroll through the fields
And sing the praises of positivity
Can lead to dim spirits and a lack of laughter

"Good ol' Grandpa," sighed Jake. "Always the poet."

"I guess we'll have to think about it..." Belle was interrupted by her phone ringing. Pulling the device out of her coat pocket, she answered it.

"Belle, where are you?" Her mother's voice was frantic.

"I'm at Frost Manor. What's wrong?"

"Your sister is about to have the baby. Her and Monty are at the hospital now. He just phoned and said the baby should be here within the hour," exclaimed her mother.

Excitement crashed over her like a tidal wave. This was the best news she had heard all month. "I'm on my way." Hanging up the phone, she turned to Jake. "My sister is going to have her baby. I have to go. I'll think about the riddle and see if I come up with anything, and you can think of some possible answers too." She took a picture of the note with her phone and then handed Jake the paper.

"Just what I wanted to do today," replied Jake sarcastically. "I might even put this candle in the window. I'll never understand why this man was so hung up on Christmas."

"Don't worry about it. I can do the thinking for both of us," Belle said as she walked over to the door.

"No, I'll see what I can think of. I must admit, I am a bit curious where all of these clues lead to."

Belle turned and saw a flicker of amusement in his sparkling emerald eyes. She felt a magnetic pull tugging at her to move closer to him and she gripped the door frame with all her might. Her heart thumped erratically in her chest as she tore her eyes away from him.

I shouldn't be feeling like this. "I have to go. I'll be in touch." Belle hurried outside to her car, her flushed cheeks cooling down in the wintry atmosphere.

"Belle!" She turned to see Donato jogging over to her.

"I'm sorry, Donato. I have to go. Josie is about to have her baby."

"I won't keep you. I have good news." Placing a hand on her shoulder, Donato whispered in her ear, "Jake gave us a check to pay for the whole job. He doesn't want you to know he paid for it. He told me just to tell you everything has been covered. But I figured you would want to know."

A smile crept across Belle's face. It was the first time she had heard someone use Jake's real name and not the Beast. "Thank you for telling me."

Getting into her car, she started the engine. She thought about Jake's kind gesture as she pulled out of Frost Manor and headed down the road. Maybe Jake was more like his grandfather than she had originally thought.

CHAPTER 14

Anticipation and nervousness could be felt throughout the waiting room in the maternity ward at White Bridge Hospital. Belle glanced around at the white walls. People sat nearby in cushioned plastic chairs, waiting to hear the news about the arrival of their newest family member. Magazines and outdated newspapers lay scattered along the small center tables. The faint aroma of coffee from the Keurigs stashed in the corner wafted around the space. Large windows obscured by blinds offered glimpses to the outside world. The ticking of the clock on the nearby wall was a constant reminder that time was moving at a snail's pace.

The birthing center was decorated with Christmas cheer, from garlands to wreaths to faux trees scattered about. The decorations made Belle think of Frost Manor. She wished there was some way to convince Jake to bring the mansion back to its former glory, but she knew it was a sensitive topic for him. The hard cushion was starting to hurt her butt. She uncrossed and recrossed her legs.

"I wish they would update us," Belle's mother whispered. Her parents sat on a couch a few feet from Belle.

"I'm sure we'll hear something soon," Monty's mother replied who sat across from them with her husband.

Reaching into her coat pocket, Belle pulled out her phone and looked at the photo of the note.

Dashing through life
can leave one unfulfilled
Forgetting to stroll through the fields
And sing the praises of positivity
Can lead to dim spirits and a lack of laughter

It seemed Sam, the poet, was advising her to take more time to enjoy life. She snorted. How she wished she had gotten that advice ten years ago. As she studied the photo, she realized there was something different about the writing in this note. Moving her fingers on the screen, she zoomed in. Some of the words were written in darker ink. She squinted. Dashing, one, fields, sing, spirits, and laughter had all been written in a bold font.

Why are these words printed darker than the others? There must be some significance.

"Nilsen and Winters families." A voice called.

Belle's thoughts were interrupted as a nurse came into the waiting room. A friendly smile crossed the older woman's exhausted face and she wiped her hand on her blue scrubs.

"That's us." Belle's mother rose to her feet.

"Everything went well with the delivery. You'll be able to see her soon. She had a healthy little girl about ten minutes ago." The nurse gave them a parting grin and disappeared back down the hall.

Excitement filled the air as the families embraced each other. Twenty-minutes later Monty appeared. Everyone hugged and congratulated him.

"Follow me. It's time for our baby to meet her family." Monty linked arms with Belle's mother and his mother and led them down the corridor. The men followed behind.

Belle was about to join when she heard a loud clatter.

An elderly woman had dropped her keys along with a stack of papers near the water cooler. The other people in the waiting room ignored the old lady. Belle felt sympathy for the woman's predicament.

"Are you alright?" Belle walked over to her and stooped down to pick up the fallen papers.

"Oh dear, how clumsy am I?" The white-haired lady touched Belle's arm affectionately. As Belle handed over the papers, she got a good look at the woman's face. Her skin was like parchment etched with a lifetime of stories. Wisps of ivory hair framed her face and drew attention to her gray eyes that sparkled with mystery. A long purple peacoat clothed her plump frame and a pair of heels and gloves completed the outfit. She exuded a comforting warmth that reminded Belle of her grandmother.

Dashing through the snow, in a one-horse open sleigh, o'er the field we go...

"That's my phone! Who's calling me?" The woman rummaged through the black bag hanging from her forearm. "Where is that darn thing?"

Dashing through the snow, in a one-horse open sleigh, o'er the fields we go... The Christmas music continued to play from inside her purse.

Belle stared at the woman's rosy face then turned her attention to the lady's gloved hand that emerged from the bag. Pressing the side of the phone, the elder silenced the tune.

"Thank you, dear." The lines in the woman's face deepened as a smile spread across her cheeks. She took the papers and keys and shoved them into her bag. "I do love Christmas carols. Such a joyous time of year. Have a Merry Christmas!" She walked toward the elevator, slinging her bag over her shoulder.

Belle watched the elevator doors close. As she headed to Josie's room, she couldn't shake the feeling of how much the woman had reminded her of her grandma. Also, she couldn't get the Christmas carol out of her head.

Dashing through the snow... Dashing? Wait a minute.

Belle paused and pulled up the picture of the note in her phone. The darkened print leaped out at her. Dashing, one, fields, sing, spirits, and laughter were all words found in the song "Jingle Bells." Belle leaned against the wall. Could Sam be referring to the song? She began to sing the tune again in her head.

"Belle?" Her mother poked her head outside the door and grabbed her arm. "What are you doing? Come on. Josie is waiting for you. We just FaceTimed Grayson and his family. His kids are so excited to meet their baby cousin."

Belle's father stepped out of the room behind her. "We're going to take a walk downstairs to the car to get a charger for your sister's phone. Monty and his parents went downstairs to get food. Go inside and keep your sister company until we get back."

Belle stepped into the spacious room. Josie was sitting in the hospital bed with a bundle of blankets in her arms. A tiny, pink striped hat peeked over the edge.

"Josie. How are you feeling?" Belle walked over and gave her sister a hug. "Congratulations." She pulled a chair as close as she could to the bed and sat down.

"Tired. But say hello to your niece. Holly Rose." She pulled the blankets aside to reveal a tiny pink face.

Tears of joy pricked the corners of Belle's eyes. "She is precious. What a little cutie." Taking the warm little bundle from Josie, Belle cradled the infant in her arms.

Josie leaned against the back of the bed and sighed. Dark circles framed her eyes like shadows. Streaks of gray accented her hair and she managed an exhausted smile. A loose hospital gown hung limply on her frame. She turned to look at Belle. "How are you feeling?"

"I'm alright. The chill has worn off." Belle rocked the baby in her arms. She couldn't take her eyes off the perfect little face nestled in layers of blankets. "I'm sure you're exhausted."

"You have no idea. But it was worth it. Mom said you were at Frost Manor?" asked Josie.

"Yes. I was trying to figure out Sam's riddle."

"Is that the only reason?" pressed Josie.

"What are you getting at, Josie? You know I made a deal with Jake." Belle raised an eyebrow.

"Well, no one can deny Jake is very handsome, even if he is a beast," chuckled Josie. "I've seen him on the rare occasion that he comes to town. He's very handsome and he keeps himself in good shape. It's a shame he's so miserable."

Belle laughed. "Josie, I'm trying to get my life together. I'm not worried about dating anyone right now."

"But you're the only one Jake has allowed to enter the manor since Sam died," Josie insisted, rubbing her temples. "That has to mean something."

"It means he's sticking to the deal we made," Belle answered, shaking her head. "Besides, I could never date someone who hates Christmas."

"Belle, it's been two years since you broke up with Pax. We all want to see you with someone who loves you as much as we do. You'll get your own place and a new job. But in the meantime, you deserve to be happy."

"We're back." Belle's mother interrupted their conversation as she entered the room.

Belle handed the baby back to Josie, and watched her family swoon over the newborn. An emptiness filled her soul. At her age, she should be celebrating happy moments like her sister and brother, but instead she sat here with no idea of where her life was headed.

CHAPTER 15

Belle leaned against her car and admired the magnificent job Donato and his crew had done. The new windows sparkled in the morning sunlight. However, the job was tainted by the glaring green and red spray paint that stuck out like a sore thumb on the house and garage. Thankfully, tomorrow the graffiti would finally be removed.

The repeated use of the word 'beast' bothered Belle. Was Jake really a beast or was he a broken person who had allowed his pain to turn him into someone he wasn't? She longed to know the circumstances that surrounded Jake's dislike towards Christmas. As she walked toward the house, she wondered what Jake thought of the widely-used nickname. While his temperament could be erratic, she didn't really think he was a beast.

She was a few feet from the front entrance when the door swung open and Jake appeared. A look of confusion crossed his face.

"What are you doing here?" He held the door open for her.

"What are you talking about? I come here every morning. It's part of our deal." Belle replied as she tried not to stare at how nice his gray sweatshirt and joggers molded to his body.

"Your sister had a baby yesterday. Shouldn't you be with her?" He closed the door as Belle stepped into the warm foyer.

"Josie is getting discharged this afternoon. I'll go see her later. She and Monty are still adjusting to being new parents. I don't want to intrude." Belle knew her answer was half true. Her obligations at Frost Manor were a distraction from the disappointment she felt about her life.

"How's the baby?" Jake asked as he walked to the kitchen.

"She's absolutely adorable." Belle opened her phone and showed him a picture she had taken of her niece. "Her name is Holly Rose."

Jake paused to look at the photo, and a small smile spread across his face. "She is precious and of course your family would pick a Christmas name."

Belle smiled at his comment. "I forgot to tell you, the graffiti removal company will be here tomorrow. I got the confirmation on my phone last night."

Jake opened the dishwasher and placed the dishes into the machine. "Finally. It irks my nerves to see that nasty name written all over Grandpa's house."

"What do you need me to do today?" Belle asked.

Jake closed the dishwasher door and pressed the button. "The solarium needs cleaning. I thought we could do it together."

"The solarium? You mean the forbidden room?" Belle joked.

"That's a little dramatic don't you think, Belle? The room is no longer forbidden," Jake replied as he walked down the hall. Belle followed him to the west side of the house where the doors were already open and waiting for them. She looked around the clean space.

"What do we need to do? The place already looks spotless," Belle asked as she looked around.

"Everything is a bit overgrown. We need to water the roses and plants, prune them, sweep the floor, dust, and clean off the furniture," Jake replied.

"I can prune the roses," Belle offered. "When I was younger, my grandma and I used to trim all of the roses outside Sam's house."

Jake grabbed a watering can that had been placed against the wall. "There are some gloves and needle-nose snippers in the empty pot by the door."

Belle put the gloves on her hands. After grabbing the pliers, she sat down next to an orange rose bush. She moved her hands through the plant, removing any of the dead leaves that had fallen off and gotten caught in the stems.

Silence filled the room as they worked together like a well-oiled machine. Jake watered the plants on one side of the octagonal room while Belle pruned the roses on the other. She was in the middle of trimming a purple rose bush, when the sparkle from the vase on the coffee table caught her eye. She stared at the black rose with petals the color of death. Curiosity took hold of her, she needed to know the story behind this rose. Belle opened her mouth to ask about it when Jake spoke. "I'm sure this isn't how you planned to spend your vacation." His muscles flexed as he lifted the watering can.

"What?" Belle turned to him.

"From work?" Jake tilted the can letting a stream of water shower the parlor palm. "I assumed with the approaching holiday, you must have vacation time since you're able to come here every day. Unless you work nights or remotely."

"Oh." Belle closed her snippers at the base of a dead flower and cut it off. "I have the time to do this because I'm unemployed." She lowered her eyes and concentrated on the thorns poking out of the stalk, hoping he would leave the topic alone and not press further.

Jake put the watering can onto the floor and looked at her. "I thought you were an artist?"

"No. That's an old hobby. To be honest, I lost my job after Thanksgiving. For a decade, I was the curator at an art gallery in New York City. I was in the running for a big promotion but then I got laid off due to decreased funding. I let one of my friends take over the lease to my apartment and I came back here to Falls Village," Belle explained as she moved her gaze to the purple blooms.

"I used to live in New York City, too. I started my own software company and we worked with a lot of the businesses in the metro area. I run my company from here now. I'm sorry to hear about your job. That establishment was a fool to let you go. You're a very strong and talented young woman, Belle. You'll get another job."

"I'm hoping to land another opportunity in the city. Staying in Falls Village is only temporary for me right now." Belle replied as she resumed trimming the wilted bits.

"You worked in an art gallery. That makes since you're the artist behind the beautiful painting in Grandpa's study. Talent like that is hard to come by." mused Jake.

Belle felt her cheeks flush. "Thank you."

"Did you show your work in the art gallery?" Jake asked.

"No, I don't paint anymore. I haven't had the time." Belle brushed off her pants and stood up.

"That's unfortunate. I would have loved to see more of your work," noted Jake.

Belle chuckled. "My parents still have my artwork hanging all over their house. My sister and brother have some of my paintings too. There are even ones hanging in the bakery. Go get a dozen cookies sometime and you'll see more of them." She glanced around the room. "This place is so beautiful. I keep trying to remember this room, but I don't."

"My grandfather built it about ten years ago. He wanted a place to tend to his roses all year round. They were his pride and joy. I helped him design it." Jake put down the watering can and picked up a bottle of disinfectant. "I remember my grandfather telling me that your grandmother and yourself were frequent visitors here. I didn't make the connection until you told me."

"Yes, when I was younger. I was around seventeen years old the last time I spent time in this house. I wish I had spent more time here as an adult. But I don't ever remember seeing you." Belle wiped her arm across her forehead.

Jake sprayed the disinfectant onto a cloth and wiped down the furniture. "I was my grandfather's only grandchild. My parents lived out of state and I rarely saw him. My grandfather and my father didn't have the best relationship, but I talked to Grandpa all the time on the phone. After my deployment, I started to visit him more. We grew close. But I rarely went into town; I mostly stayed here in the house working on my business. That's why nobody knows me or remembers me. I tend to avoid people. I like to keep to myself."

Belle tossed a perished rose head into the nearby garbage. She took off her gloves and threw them onto the ground. Her hands were sweaty and the gloves were too bulky. "Why didn't you want me in this room? It seems to hold a lot of significance to Sam."

Darkness crept into Jake's eyes. "That's water under the bridge now, Belle."

Belle nodded and continued to pick through a rose bush with red blooms. Something sharp pricked her skin. "Ouch!" She pulled her hand away. A dark drop of blood beaded on the tip of her fingers.

"What happened?" Jake rushed to her side.

"I'm fine. I wasn't watching what I was doing, and I stabbed my finger on the thorn," groaned Belle.

"Why aren't you wearing gloves?" Jake scolded as he picked up the pair she'd discarded.

"They're too big and my palms were sweaty." Belle rolled her eyes when Jake grabbed her hand to look at the cut. "Jake, it's nothing."

"It's not nothing. You're bleeding!" His hold on her hand was firm, but gentle.

Belle's gaze met his and they locked eyes for a moment. Belle's heart pounded a frantic rhythm against her ribs. Jake broke the stare and looked down at her finger. "It looks like a papercut. Those nasty things bleed forever." He took a tissue from his pocket, and carefully pressed it to the wound. "We need to get this cleaned up." He took her by the hand, and led her out of the solarium to the kitchen.

"I can do it," Belle insisted as Jake held her hand under the faucet and turned on the water. He poured a bottle of peroxide over the cut. Belle inhaled sharply as her skin tingled and burned. Jake continued his work until the cut was clean and covered with a bandage.

"Thank you," Belle said, looking down at her wrapped finger.

"You're welcome." Jake washed his hands and dried them. "Did you decipher the note you found under the candle?" He reached into his pocket and pulled out the riddle, placing it onto the granite counter.

Belle furrowed her brow in confusion. "I thought you said it was a waste of time?"

Jake shrugged. "It is. But it doesn't mean I'm not curious to know the meaning behind my grandfather's scavenger hunt. It feels like a piece of him is still here."

"I think that Sam is referring to the Christmas carol, *Jingle Bells*."

"*Jingle Bells*?" The all-familiar sour expression returned to Jake's face.

"Yes. If you look at the note you can see the words dashing, one, fields, sing, spirits, and laughter were all written in a darker ink. Those are words from the song." Belle explained as she pointed to each of the words.

A small smile appeared on Jake's lips. "*Jingle Bells* was my grandmother's favorite Christmas carol."

"Then that's the answer to the riddle," Belle declared.

"But the song isn't directing us anywhere. It just says 'o'er the fields we go'." Jake rolled his eyes.

"Maybe it's directing us to the Christmas tree fields?" Belle suggested.

"I walk through the fields all the time and I've never seen anything unusual there. But I can take Jingle for a walk and look again. Would you like to join us?" Jake asked as he threw the bloody towel into the garbage.

"Yes, I would. But can we make it tomorrow? I need to head to Josie's house to prepare for her arrival from the hospital. We are having a family gathering," replied Belle.

"Tomorrow it is. In the meantime, I'll look over the security footage and fly the drone around the outermost lots."

"Let me know if you find anything." Belle took her coat off the hanger.

"I won't be able to update you unless you give me your number," Jake suggested slyly. "You know, for Christmas-riddle-related business of course."

Belle hid a smile and held out her hand for his phone. After punching her number into his contacts, she handed the phone back to him. "I'll see you tomorrow." She walked to the door and paused. "Jake?"

"Yes?"

The words felt stuck on her tongue. She wanted to ask him why he hated Christmas so much but she didn't have the heart to upset him.

"Belle?"

"Um, have a good afternoon, Jake." Belle gave him a parting smile before ducking out the front door.

As she approached her car, she hoped the wind would shake the feelings that were taking hold of her. Could Jake ever love Christmas again or would he forever be a beastly Scrooge about her favorite holiday?

CHAPTER 16

"Josie's out of the hospital. She and Monty should be here any minute with the baby," Belle's mother exclaimed. Her voice trembled with excitement as she placed the last covered dish in the fridge.

Belle, her parents, Grayson, and his family had spent the entire afternoon at Josie and Monty's house cleaning the place from top to bottom. Her mother had made enough food to feed an army. Grayson and his family had brought over balloons and decorations, and Belle had gotten the flowers and desserts. Tying a ribbon around the last vase, Belle finished arranging the floral display on the dining room table.

"We need to hurry," called her mother.

"Relax Mom, the house looks amazing." Belle replied. She leaned against the wall and stretched her arms over her head to release the tension in her shoulders.

Grayson slid into one of the dining room chairs and leaned on the table. "So, Belle. How do you like working for the Beast? I've made Logan, Aviva, and Ciella feel guilty about it every day."

Something in his voice told her he was looking for a specific answer. She wondered if he had talked to Josie about her and Jake being a couple.

"It's not so bad," she admitted.

"I drove by Frost Manor yesterday. I saw the windows had been fixed. When does your prison sentence end?" asked Grayson.

"The graffiti removal company is coming tomorrow. But I may continue going to help spruce up some of the rooms in the manor," Belle fiddled with the ribbon.

Grayson gave her a puzzled look. "The kids didn't mess up the rooms in the house. Why would you do that?"

"I don't mind. I always loved that house. It has been so long since I was last there that I feel like I'm exploring the place for the first time. You wouldn't believe all the changes Sam has made in the past few years," Belle replied.

"You are a strong woman, Belle. If I fell in a pond on the Beast's property, I would have run for the hills and never gone back. He should have released you from the agreement to avoid his own legal troubles."

"I'm the one who was trespassing where I shouldn't have been. Besides, I'm trying to figure out the meaning behind Sam's gift. Jake's curious too. He's been helping me." Belle readjusted one of the roses in the vase.

"Oh, really?" Grayson's eyes widened. "You're working with the Beast now?"

"He isn't that bad once you get to know him."

"I'm sure he's quite enticing to the ladies, but remember: every beast has claws, sis. Be careful. I don't want to see you get hurt." Grayson touched her shoulder affectionately as he got up from the table.

A ding sounded on Belle's phone. Looking down, she saw it was a message from Jake.

Hi. Sorry to bother you. I just wanted to let you know I figured out the meaning of the riddle. I'll explain tomorrow. Have a good afternoon.

A jolt of adrenaline coursed through her as her thumb hovered over the screen. Should she text back? Belle chided herself on the rollercoaster of emotions coursing through her, all sparked by a simple string of words. *What am I doing? I can't be fawning over a beast. I need to get my life together.*

"They're here!" Aviva's excited voice called from the living room. She was on lookout duty. "Everyone, take your positions."

Belle clicked the side button and let the screen fade to black. Walking into the living room, Belle made it just in time to shout "Surprise," with the rest of her family as Josie and Monty entered the home with Holly in her carrier.

Josie's eyes brimmed with tears. "This is beautiful. Thank you so much everyone."

"We won't stay long," Belle's mother said, giving Josie a hug. "We wanted you to come home to a full refrigerator and a clean house.

"Thanks Mom." Josie hugged her.

"Anna, you're the best." Monty joined in the hug.

Belle's mind wandered back to the emptiness she'd felt in the hospital, a stark contrast to the cheerful chatter that surrounded her now. When would her life regain its meaning?

CHAPTER 17

"Where are we going?" Belle stood on the back steps sandwiched between the door and the screen.

"We're going to the equipment barn," replied Jake as he strolled across the snowy yard.

"The graffiti removal company will be here soon," Belle called after him.

"As soon as they pull up, I'll know." Jake waved his phone in the air before shoving it back into his coat pocket. "Come on."

The frigid Vermont air hit her face as soon as she stepped into the yard. The breeze chased away any remaining sleepiness, and brought the smoky smell from the many chimneys in the area. Her boots crunched in the newly fallen snow, leaving a trail of footprints behind her. The Frost property stretched for miles. Horses with blankets on their bodies were outside in the corral, and cows shuffled around, rooting for any remaining grass. Bare trees were coated in icy attire, leaving them breathtakingly beautiful against the blue sky.

"What's in the equipment barn?" Belle asked through chattering teeth as her breath puffed before her.

"I spent all night thinking about the note. It never states a location. However, the riddle does give a means of transportation. The singer is traveling by sleigh, which means we need to find a sleigh," Jake declared.

"Where are we going to find a sleigh?" Belle furrowed her brow.

"I guess we're going to have to call up Santa Claus and see if he will lend us his." Jake joked as he shot her a smirk over his shoulder.

"Very funny," replied Belle. She brought her scarf to her mouth and nose to block out the wind.

The equipment barn wasn't too far from the other barns. The structure was massive and painted bright red with white trim. It took all of Jake's strength to open the doors due to ice and lack of use.

"My grandparents had a sleigh. I remember going for rides with them when I was little." Jake reached over and flipped the switch as they stepped inside. The overhead lights suspended from the wooden rafters flickered and buzzed.

An earthy smell filled Belle's nose as she looked at the large tractors lined against the wall, along with multiple mowers. Trimmers and wheelbarrows filled the aisle. Shovels, racks, and other garden tools glinted in the filtered sunlight from their positions on sturdy hooks.

Jake walked to the far end of the barn and disappeared behind a giant tractor. "Here it is."

Belle rounded the side of the machine to find Jake pulling a tarp off a forgotten object in the corner. It was a sleigh.

The sleigh was a handcrafted antique. Its vibrant red exterior was accented with gold trim and intricate yellow metalwork. The exquisite heirloom boasted a spacious interior, complete with a crimson bench seat and ample storage behind it. Silver street runners finished the elegant design.

"It looks just like Santa's sleigh." Belle breathed, she could feel Christmas magic radiating off the exterior.

"I think that was the idea." Jake ran his hand along the gold railing on the upper part of the sleigh. "My grandfather made it for my grandmother. They used to ride around the tree lots and pretend to be Mr. and Mrs. Claus. They always got a good laugh out of seeing the looks on the children's faces." Jake paused, and a smile spread over his face as if he was remembering a happier time he had long forgotten. Light from the large windows drew attention to his high cheekbones and chiseled jaw. Sadness crossed his face as he continued to stare at the sleigh. Before she realized it, Belle had placed her gloved hand over Jake's. He looked down at their hands then at her. Belle felt herself drawing closer to him. At the last second Jake pulled away. "Anyway, this is what Grandpa must have been referring to in the note," he added.

Belle cleared her throat and walked behind the sleigh to escape the tension. "It's in incredible condition."

"It needs a little dusting and cleaning to make it really shine. It's been sitting here for a while," Jake replied.

"But what exactly are we looking for?" Belle stood on her tiptoes to peer inside the spacious seat. She gripped the side of the sleigh and leaned over, examining the cherry-colored interior. There was nothing. Moving to the seat, she stuck her hand underneath. She came up empty.

"I'm not sure. I wonder..." Jake squatted down to the cement floor and laid on his back, inching his way underneath the sleigh. Pulling his phone out of his pocket, he turned on the flashlight. "There it is."

"What did you find?" Belle came around the other side as Jake crawled back out.

He handed her an index card. Belle recognized Sam's cursive script. There was no riddle this time. Instead, a mixture of numbers and letters scrawled across the paper provided even more confusion.

A.C.C.

C.D.

19121843

Jake stood up and brushed the dust off his jeans. Then he leaned over her shoulder to read the note. "What does it mean?" he asked.

"I don't know. A code or something?"

"I think I prefer Grandpa's riddles to whatever this is." Jake pointed to the numbers. "Could this be a code to a safe?"

"If that's the case then what do the letters mean?" Belle asked. "A code to a safe is usually only numbers."

"Not necessarily, but maybe they're abbreviations for the place we need to go to."

"Did your grandfather have a lock box in a bank or a storage unit or something like that?" Belle took a picture of the note with her phone.

Jake shook his head. "Not that I know of but this property is massive. Why would he keep something in the bank or a storage unit when he has enough land and a house to hide anything he wanted?"

"None of this makes sense." Belle sighed.

A loud ding from Jake's pocket stopped any further discussion. He took out his phone and a smile broke out over his face. "The graffiti removal guys are here. Thank God! Now I can finally get this ugly spray paint off my house." He started to head to the door.

"Jake, wait," Belle called after him. She needed an answer to the question that had been gnawing at her for days. It might not be the best time but she needed to get it off her chest.

"Yes, Belle." He turned to look at her, his silhouette framed in the sunlight.

"Why do you hate Christmas so much?" Belle blurted out the words. She wanted to go into more detail, but she hesitated.

Jake's shoulders sagged. "I don't hate Christmas, Belle," he insisted. Then he retreated into the winter sunlight, leaving Belle alone with a cryptic note, and a growing list of unanswered questions.

CHAPTER 18

Cursive script laughed at Belle's inability to decipher its meaning as she stood in the barn alone after Jake's departure. She read the note again.

A.C.C.

C.D.

19121843

"What does this even mean? Why are you doing this to me, Sam?" Belle walked to the door and slid it open. The northern air rushed in. She strolled across the snow-covered yard and re-entered the house. Minutes later she stood in the solarium as the smell of roses filled her nose. This place reminded her of Sam. His memory was associated with his love of roses. The beautiful bushes that filled the space spoke volumes about his dedication to things that mattered to him. Belle plopped down into one of the wicker chairs. The solarium was becoming her haven of peace. She understood Sam's intention behind building this magnificent place. It was a paradise inside his home for him to retreat to whenever he wanted.

As she placed the note on the coffee table, her eyes fell on the black rose. The depressing flower sat in its vase on top of a stack of three books. Belle's fingertips traced the delicate petals. *Why would Jake keep a black rose in the center of all this beauty?*

"This is where you went," a voice rang out. Belle turned to see Jake standing in the doorway, leaning against the frame. "This place has always been a favorite with the ladies." A smirk crept across his face as he walked to the large window. He placed his hand on the glass and looked out across the fields.

Belle felt her curiosity peek and a bitter taste rose in her mouth. What ladies could Jake be referring to? She tried to brush off the comment but inside she wanted to know more.

She forced a smile and blurted out, "I think Frost Manor needs a Christmas tree." Belle knew she shouldn't say such things but his reference to other women had her feeling a little envious. Even though she knew they weren't a couple, the more time they spent together, the more she saw that they weren't so different after all.

Jake turned away from the window and looked at her. "This again?"

Belle chose her words carefully. "You say you don't hate Christmas, and yet this place reeks of anti-Christmas vibes. I know you don't want to decorate the manor but maybe you can find it in your heart to get a tree. It is one of the essential pieces of the holiday season. Besides, this house is so big you wouldn't even notice it. You have acres and acres of beautiful pines waiting for the opportunity to shine bright in your living room. I can get the tree and decorate it. It would be a testament to Sam's legacy."

Jake folded his arms. "Do you know the size of the tree you would need for the living room? It would be way too big and heavy for one person."

"I'll figure it out. Can we please have a tree?"

"I supposed I can live with one tree," sighed Jake. "But I'll have to help you. The men are almost done with the job. Once the graffiti is removed, I'll attach the utility sled to the snowmobile. Then we can go to the fields and get a tree. But you're decorating it on your own. Don't drag me into that. I won't do it."

Belle jumped to her feet. A smile spread across her face. "Thank you, Jake."

Jake nodded, then departed from the room like the north wind.

Belle felt a tingle of excitement spread throughout her body. "Yes!" She pumped her fist in the air. She never expected Jake to agree to a tree but he did. Maybe if she played her cards right, she could have the entire Frost Manor decked out in holiday cheer before Christmas.

CHAPTER 19

A soft crunch beneath Belle's feet was the only sound as she walked around the side of Frost Manor. The crisp cold air bit at her face and her breath formed visible clouds. Every tree, shrub, and fence post was adorned with a delicate frosting of ice crystals. The side yard was silent and full of untouched beauty. Making her way to the front of the house, Belle stopped and stared at the mansion. The marks of cruelty were gone, and the graffiti-free home glistened in the afternoon sun. Feet from her, Jake nodded in approval. He smiled. "I can't even begin to describe how nice it is not to see the word 'beast' written everywhere." Waving for her to follow him, they walked over to the garage. As Jake punched a code into the keypad of the multi-car garage, Belle wondered about the next clue.

"Are you ready?" Jake's voice brought Belle's attention back to the task at hand. One of the doors retracted backward to reveal dirt bikes, quads, snowmobiles, jet skis, and motorcycles. Stepping inside, Jake walked over to a cabinet door and took out two full-face helmets. He tossed one to her, pulling the other one over his head. "Put that on."

Belle placed the covering over her head and pulled the glass shield down over her face. The snowy world around her was immediately tinted in a dim glow. As she finished fastening the chin strap, an engine roared to life. Two bright headlights flooded the garage. A royal blue snowmobile pulled onto the driveway. A long utility sled was attached to the back.

Jake sat on the saddle-like seat and gestured for her to join him. Belle rested her hand on his shoulder, and swung her leg over, straddling the seat. Once her arms were wrapped around his torso, Belle felt the machine leap into motion, speeding toward the tree lot.

As the snowmobile glided under the arched entryway, Belle turned to see the Wishing Bell standing proud in the center of the ghostly area. She hoped one day it would be surrounded by people again.

Jake took them past the Christmas tree fields and deeper into the property. The pines whirled past Belle in a green blur. With each maneuver, Belle could feel Jake's muscles rippling through his coat. The warmth of his back against her chest felt comforting, and she leaned into him.

Stop feeling like this. Remember, he was going to throw your nieces and nephew in jail, her inner thoughts chided her. Yet she couldn't help but feel a mutual attraction every time they were near each other.

The snowmobile sped between two holly trees into a clearing. Jake stopped the machine, turned off the engine, and removed his helmet. Belle unfastened her helmet and placed it on the seat behind her. While fixing her curls, she looked around at the small clearing filled with blue spruces. The needled branches were highlighted with shades of colors that none of the other lots had.

"Where are we?" she asked as she got off the snowmobile.

"This is a special Christmas tree grove that my grandfather planted for our family. Since many people come from miles around to get trees from our lots, Grandpa wanted a special place where his kids and grandkids could go to find the perfect tree."

Belle turned to him. "I don't mean to pry Jake, but I don't understand. You partook in so much Christmas tradition growing up. I see your face light up whenever you speak of the memories. What changed?"

"You wouldn't understand." Jake set his jaw tightly as he opened the storage compartment on the snowmobile and took out a saw.

Feeling bold, Belle walked over to him, and touched his arm. "Try me. I would understand."

Silence passed between them as they looked into each other's eyes. Belle could feel his pain. For a moment, she thought he would finally open up, but he turned away from her and walked toward the trees.

"I know this is your house and your property, but it's not fair," Belle called to him.

Jake stopped but he didn't turn around. "Fair?"

"It's not fair that because of your personal feelings, you have to take away something we consider a tradition for decades in Falls Village. People love getting their trees from these lots. They love seeing Frost Manor decorated. They believe in the Wishing Bell, even if you don't. Christmas is a time of hope, and it's a time to believe even when you feel like giving up. I spent ten years of my life pouring my blood, sweat, and tears into being a curator at the art gallery. I didn't even come home for Thanksgiving because I thought I was going to get a promotion, and instead, they laid me off." She felt tears prick at the corners of her eyes. She had no idea why she felt so emotional. But all the feelings she had been bottling for weeks were coming forth, like opening a soda can after it had been shaken violently. "I have no job, I lost my apartment, I have nothing. I thought I had my whole life planned out, but everything got turned upside down. The day we had our argument on the front porch, I had come to Frost Manor to make a wish on the Wishing Bell. I have no idea who I am anymore or where my life is going. I believe in the magic of the bell. Everyone believes in the magic. Sam shared his fortune with all of us, and he would want you to do the same."

Jake's shoulders slumped and he clutched the saw tighter. "You are so set on me acting like my grandfather. You want me to be responsible for the rest of the world's happiness by opening this Christmas nightmare again."

"That's because I know you're just like him, Jake. I don't care what everyone in Falls Village thinks of you. I know you're not a beast. Your eyes hold the same kindness as your grandfather. Maybe opening the manor is just what you need to take the horrible memories you have about Christmas, and turn them into something happy. There are two weeks until Christmas, and it's been almost a year since your grandfather left us. Don't you think this would be a great way to honor his legacy? You taking away the holiday that defined Sam, it's like he never existed. What if you opened Frost Manor one last time for everyone to say goodbye, and then you never have to do it again?"

Jake shook his head. "I don't want to talk about this right now, Belle."

Belle sighed and shoved her hands in her pockets. "Alright, Jake." She pushed past him and headed into the pine trees.

"I know what it's like to have your life all planned out, and then it doesn't turn out the way you wanted." Jake called after her.

Belle turned around and looked at him.

"I don't want to argue with you. I'm getting a Christmas tree to spruce up the manor a bit, and let's leave it at that," Jake pleaded.

Belle looked down at the snow-covered ground and nodded. Getting a tree was supposed to be a happy moment, not one full of arguments. "I think we should get that tree over there." She pointed to a narrow-shaped spruce at the edge of the grove.

Jake wrinkled his nose. "What? I thought you were supposed to be an expert. That tree isn't big enough. The bigger ones are this way."

They strolled through the clearing and Jake pointed out some pines he thought would be suitable for the living room. As they commented about each tree, the tension from their earlier conversation dissipated.

"I think this is the one." Belle stopped in front of a tall blue spruce that was a vision of festive elegance. The plump tree had a lush triangular shape with needles of deep green and a sturdy trunk. The branches were evenly spaced and perfect for hanging multiple ornaments and lights throughout. The crisp scent of pine needles filled the air around them.

"I couldn't agree more." Jake knelt down into the snow and crawled under the boughs. He placed the shiny saw against the straight trunk and moved the blade back and forth.

A rhythmic, high-pitched screech sounded in the still air as the teeth bit into the wood, spraying flecks of sawdust across the snow. The pine wobbled back and forth. As Jake made the final cut, the tree tilted sideways and fell to the ground. Jake got to his feet and looked down at the spruce's boughs with a proud smile. "It's been a very long time since I cut down a Christmas tree." He moved to grab one of the thick limbs that were attached to the truck. Belle took another branch, and together they dragged the tree over to the utility sled, placing it onto the bed. Jake fastened the rope around the pine to hold it in place and then started the snowmobile.

The drive back was silent apart from the noisy engine. Belle wished Jake would open up to her. She wanted to know what was causing him so much pain. If he wasn't trapped within his own walls, she might be able to get through to him.

Fifteen minutes later, they were back at Frost Manor. Jake pulled the snowmobile parallel to the kitchen door.

"I know there's an old tree stand somewhere. I think it's in the closet next to the kitchen. Wait here." Jake got off the snowmobile and stomped his boots on the stoop. He disappeared inside for a few minutes. "I found it," he called as he opened the screen door and pressed a button on the bottom to hold it in place. "Let's get this beast inside."

Belle smirked at his choice of words as she took off her helmet and placed it on the seat. Then she walked over to where Jake had untied the rope around the pine and was standing near the trunk.

"I'll help."

"No, it's fine. I don't want you to get hurt." Jake circled the utility sled. Belle could see him strategizing how he was going to move this large tree by himself.

"I'll help you. It was my idea to get the tree in the first place." She positioned herself at the top of the tree.

A faint smile twitched on Jake's lips. "You don't ever take no for an answer, do you? Alright. Lift on three. One...two...three."

Together they hoisted the tree onto their shoulders. Belle would never admit how difficult it was to maneuver the tree into the house. The weight of the pine dug into her shoulders. The branches brushed against her face as she tried to keep it upright. Belle had to keep readjusting her grip as they walked up the back steps and into the kitchen. Her arms ached from the strain and her fingers felt numb. Sweat prickled on her forehead as she wrestled with the unwieldy mass.

Jake had set up the tree stand in the living room. He guided the pine into the stand and locked it into place. Belle sighed in relief and looked back at the trail of pine needles that was scattered across the floor. The strong earthy scent from the tree filled the room. Together they stared at the massive tree that stood before them. Belle placed her hands on her hips in contentment. "It looks stunning."

"I guess." Jake walked over and closed the kitchen door. "I thought I would never see a Christmas tree in this place again." He opened the closet and took out a vacuum. "Are you doing anything tonight?"

"No, why?" Belle grabbed a broom and started sweeping the needles into a pile.

"I was thinking, if you were free, we could decorate the tree together." Jake started the vacuum, keeping his eyes looking down.

A flicker of surprise crossed Belle's face. Wasn't he the one who'd been adamant he wasn't going to decorate?

"And we can try to figure out what the letters and numbers on the note mean," Jake added quickly.

"I'd love to," she replied over the loud buzz of the vacuum. She wasn't going to question his change of heart.

Jake turned off the machine. "Excellent. I'll make us dinner, too. You can head to the attic on the third floor. That's where the ornaments are. I'll grab more lights and ribbon from the garage after I finish." He restarted the vacuum and went back to work.

Belle smiled as she headed down the corridor to the attic stairs. Jake was unpredictable but something about that thrilled her. The attic door creaked open, revealing a world of shadows. Belle walked up the stairs and stepped into the large space. She pulled the chain that turned on the lights. The brightness revealed centuries worth of history before her. Sunrays filtered through a small window. The air was thick with the scent of old paper and forgotten memories. Boxes and trunks were stacked against the wall. Old clothes racks, a rocking chair, mirrors, and dressers were scattered about. It looked like it had been a while since anyone had set foot in this place.

Belle scanned the boxes, looking for one labeled 'ornaments.' Sam's familiar handwriting was on many of the boxes, but none of them had what she needed. The side of her hip rammed into a desk. "Ouch!" One of the drawers was ajar and hung awkwardly. As she went to close it, the glimmer of a picture frame caught her eye.

What's this?" She took out an object nestled among the various items.

The wooden frame held a picture of a woman with long, wavy blonde hair and sunkissed skin. She wore an off-the-shoulder top and her head was tilted, giving the camera a sultry expression. The glass that shielded the frame had been smashed, and chunks were missing. In addition, long cracks that looked like a spider's web slithered across the image. Belle turned the picture over. Pieces of glass fell from the frame and sprinkled the floor. On the back, words had been written in a fancy script: Forever, my love.

"Did you find the ornaments?" Jake's voice called up to her from the bottom of the stairs.

"I'm still looking," Belle answered as she clutched the frame in her hands.

"They should be there. Hang on. I'll come help you." His boots thumped on the stairs.

Belle placed the frame facedown on top of the desk. She had a feeling she shouldn't tell Jake. The smashed photo had been placed in the drawer for a reason.

"Wow, I haven't been in this place for a long time," he mused as he stepped into the attic. His eyes scanned the boxes. "Ah, there they are."

"How did I not see it?" Belle scratched her head.

Jake bent down and picked up a huge box near the entrance. "There are a lot of memories in this attic. Anyone can get distracted easily. Come on, let's head downstairs."

Belle nodded and followed him. As she reached the door, she took one last look at the photo frame sitting on the desk. Frost Manor held too many secrets. Instead of solving one of its riddles, she just kept finding more.

CHAPTER 20

"These decorations are so beautiful." Belle sat on the floor in front of the majestic pine. A roaring fire crackled in the background and a cardboard box was next to her. Belle held up an antique glass ornament of a prancing reindeer. Taking the trinkets out one by one, Belle lined them up on a blanket. She admired the old-fashioned craftsmanship and antique glamor. The smell of vodka sauce and warm bread filled the living room. Belle inhaled deeply, her mouth watered. She looked across the space to where Jake was busy cooking in the kitchen. The Beast of Frost Manor was proving to be a man of many talents.

"That smell is amazing," she called.

"It's one of my grandmother's recipes," he replied above the clattering of pots and pans.

Belle reached over and rubbed Jingle's head who was stretched out on his red cushion in front of the stone fireplace. Glancing up at the tree, Belle admired their work so far. They had spent the afternoon stringing the lights and ribbon. After dinner, they would start hanging the ornaments. Reaching into the box, she picked up a beautiful glass ball with frosted snowflakes. Many of the ornaments reminded her of similar trinkets she had hung on her own tree with her family.

"Alright, dinner is served," Jake announced as he carried two plates over to the table in the breakfast nook.

After washing her hands, Belle joined him. She stared in awe at the food that covered the table. "You cooked all of this?"

"Yes, my mother taught me how to cook. She said that I needed to learn to take care of myself and not rely on anyone else. For dinner tonight we have gnocchi with vodka sauce, bread, meatballs, fried calamari, and salad."

Belle's mouth watered as she looked at the creamy pink sauce with fat dumpling pasta floating around in her plate. Belle stuck her fork into the soft gnocchi and brought it to her lips. The flavors danced on her tongue as the pasta exploded in her mouth. She picked up a napkin and dabbed her face. "This is amazing. I had no idea you knew how to cook."

"I never go out to eat. I have all my groceries delivered and I make my own food. I'm not big on social interaction." Jake cut a meatball in half with his fork and popped it into his mouth.

"Why is that?" Belle asked between mouthfuls of pasta.

Jake shrugged and looked down at his food. "You know how this town feels about me. If I went out to eat, I would have everyone henpecking me about Frost Manor. I'd get question after question about why I didn't open the tree lot, why I'm not making the Wishing Bell available to the public, and why I didn't decorate the mansion. People would be giving me the evil eye wherever I went or calling me names. I've never felt welcome here. To them, I'm a beast who hates Christmas. I would rather just keep my distance and have everything I need brought to me."

"You're not a beast, Jake. Once people get to know you, they'll see what I see and realize you're a good person."

"I doubt that," Jake mumbled.

Belle was about to reply when she felt something cold press against her arm. With her fork poised before her mouth, she looked down to see Jingle pushing his big head against her forearm.

"Hey, boy, what are you doing?" she cooed.

"He wants food," chuckled Jake. "Your food is in the kitchen buddy, come on."

Jake stood up and took his half-eaten dinner with him to the kitchen. Seconds later, the splash of water and the swooshing sound of a sponge against ceramic could be heard coming from the sink.

Belle continued to shovel food into her mouth. The meal was so delicious, she found it hard to put down her fork. After finishing dinner, Belle left her plate in the kitchen and headed to the living room. Her eyes drifted over the dozens of little figures, glass balls, stockings, Santas, and reindeer that were spread across the floor. Each one was unique and carefully crafted to reflect the beauty of the season. She'd never seen a collection like this before. Taking a rag, she wiped away the dust on each ornament. Soon all the trinkets shined bright in the glow of the fireplace.

Belle stared at the tree and began to plot out where each ornament would go.

"My great-great-grandparents brought most of those ornaments over when they immigrated here from England. Throughout the decades, we kept adding to them." Jake walked into the living room holding a tray. On it were two cups of hot chocolate brimming over with marshmallows.

"You can't decorate a tree without hot cocoa." He placed the tray on the coffee table.

Belle reached over and picked up one of the mugs. "Thanks, Jake. But I don't think we have enough to decorate the tree."

"We have enough. Those are the special ornaments. While you were taking forever in the attic, I got out some of the other boxes from the garage." He nodded toward a stack in the corner. "Those are the ones..." He paused.

The ones Sam used to decorate the manor." Belle finished.

Jake nodded, picked up a red glass ornament, and fastened it to one of the middle branches.

Belle took a blue ornament and hung it on the tree. As she took a sip of her hot chocolate, she glanced at the fireplace. On the mantle was a photo of an older couple. They were dressed in elegant attire. The elderly woman wore an off-the-shoulder green gown that sparkled in the light. Her white hair was pulled up in a bun and her arms were linked with the older man. He wore a black suit and had a white beard. His appearance reminded Belle of Santa Claus.

"Is that Sam?" she asked, moving closer to the fireplace.

A smile flashed across Jake's chiseled features. "It sure is. That's Grandpa Sam and Grandma Agnes at the Christmas Gala decades ago. I think I had just been born when this photo was taken."

"They look so happy." Belle reached up and placed her fingers against the glass.

"That's my favorite photo of them. They loved the Christmas Gala. I think that was the last one they had before the Community Center burned down. It's too bad they never kept up the tradition. It sounds like it would be fun to go to something like that." Jake picked up another ornament and hung it on a lower bough. "Speaking of my grandfather, have you given any more thought to what those letters and numbers could mean?"

"I don't know." Belle walked back to the boxes of ornaments. "It could be a code or a cipher. I see you have become just as invested in this as me."

"Grandpa had a way of doing that," Jake replied as he grabbed the ladder and set it up by the tree. "If you didn't want to do something, he would find a way to entice you to do it with his puzzles and riddles." He climbed the steps and placed an ornament near the top of the tree.

Bit by bit they took turns covering the spruce with decorations. As each piece was placed on the branches, Belle felt Sam's memory coming alive and the holiday magic emerging in the manor. When the last decoration had been placed, Belle and Jake stepped back to admire their work.

"It looks gorgeous." Belle pulled her phone out of her pocket to snap a quick photo.

"One final piece." Jake reached into the box and pulled out a shimmering gold and white star. "You can't have a tree without the star. You can do the honors." He pulled the ladder closer to the tree. Grasping the side, Belle climbed to the top. Leaning over, she placed the star on the tip of the tree.

Jake turned on the lights, and the tree came to life, bathing the room in a soft, yellow glow. Smiling, Belle began a slow descent back down the ladder. As she reached the last few rungs, Jingle awoke from his nap in front of the fire and rose to his feet. He scampered under the ladder, bumping the side with his massive frame. The jolt caught Belle off guard and her feet slipped. She fell off the ladder into Jake's arms. His chest was warm against her side and his powerful embrace made her feel safe. He lowered her gently to the wood floor. His hands lingered on her arms as she regained her footing. Concern was written across his face.

"Are you alright?" he asked.

"Y-yes." Belle turned to see Jingle grab a large squeaky toy that was half-hidden under the couch. The Saint Bernard picked up the teddy bear in his mouth and shook his head.

"It's been a few years since I decorated a tree. I forgot how good it feels," Jake said.

As Belle was about to reply, Jingle lumbered back to his bed by the fire. His powerful body bumped against Belle's legs, causing her to pitch forward again into Jake's arms.

"I'm so sorry," gasped Belle, as her hands wrapped around his shoulders.

"Don't be," Jake whispered into her ear as he held her firmly in place. His hands around her waist sent a tingling sensation through her body. The ambiance of the Christmas tree, the roaring fire, and the snow falling outside the window filled the room with romantic energy.

Belle looked up at Jake. His emerald eyes held her captive as his gaze dropped to her lips. His warm hand cupped her face, and his thumb traced the curve of her jaw. Their breaths mingled as their lips were inches apart. Her heart caught in her throat as his face moved closer to hers.

Ruff! Ruff!

Belle snapped back to reality and stepped out of Jake's embrace, much to her dismay. Looking around, she saw Jingle had made a u-turn and was barking at the kitchen door.

"He wants to go outside." Jake cleared his throat and moved toward the dog in an attempt to brush off the almost-kiss as if it didn't happen. He grabbed a leash off the shelf. "Would you like to go for a nighttime stroll before you leave?"

Belle nodded, following him to the coat closet.

"Come on, Jingle." Jake stepped outside into the cool night air with the dog at his heels.

A pang of disappointment gnawed at Belle as the frigid wind nipped at her face. A part of her wished Jake had followed through with the kiss but another part of her was fearful. Romance hadn't been part of the plan when she returned to Falls Village. She was supposed to spend time with her family, find a job, and leave for New York again. She looked up at the twinkling stars sprinkled across the navy blue canvas. A crescent moon hung in the center of the sky, illuminating the snow-covered yard. The bare branches from the nearby trees were etched against the dark sky like dancing skeletons. The scene was breathtaking. "I forgot how well you can see the stars in Vermont. In New York City, you never see them."

"I remember. There was never a view like this." Jake's breath puffed from his mouth as he watched Jingle lumber over to a nearby tree. "Let's go for a walk. Jingle will come when he's finished."

Belle fell into step with Jake. She shoved her hands deep into her pockets to keep the chill from settling into her bones. She glanced at Jake who seemed to be in his own world. His shoulders were hunched as if he held the weight of the world on his back. Her heart fluttered with excitement when she realized he was walking her toward the Wishing Bell. The silver beauty gleamed in the moonlight.

"I really used to like this bell," Jake said as they stood before the precious heirloom. He seemed to be speaking more to himself than to her. "I used to be as excited as everyone else to make a wish every year, until the bell let me down."

"How?" Belle looked over at him.

Jake stared at the snow and shook his head. "It doesn't matter. I made a wish and my wish didn't come true." He cleared his throat. "It was the most important thing I'd ever asked for, and when it didn't happen, it proved to me that wishes are nothing more than a fairytale. The Wishing Bell was just a gimmick to separate my family's tree farm from everyone else's."

"What did you wish for?" Belle pressed.

Jake didn't answer. He glared at the bell as if the decorative designs and gold etching were responsible for his misery.

Belle reached over and touched his arm. "I'm sorry, Jake. Maybe your wish didn't come true because you were meant for something better."

Jake looked out into the acres of pines. "I've been doing some thinking. I've been foolish to take my problems out on the town. My grandfather was known for Frost Manor. He deserves to have recognition for all the good he has done. You fulfilled your obligations and took care of the damages when you didn't have to. In return, I'll give you permission to decorate Frost Manor one last time to honor my grandfather's legacy. You have free rein, but I want no part of it."

A squeal erupted from Belle's lips as she threw her arms around Jake. "Thank you. Thank you." Jake hugged her back. "Can we open the tree lot, too?" Belle pleaded as she stepped out of the embrace. Raising an eyebrow, Jake gave her a look. "No, Belle."

"Alright. Decorating the house is fine with me." Belle did a little happy dance, jumping up and down in the snow.

"In my grandfather's study, there is a notebook with all the information about the people who helped him decorate the manor. I have to head back inside. I need to get ready for a video meeting with my investors in Tokyo." Jake puckered his lips and a loud whistle sounded. Jingle, who had been nosing around a holly bush, came racing across the yard to his side.

Belle turned back to the bell and looked at the engraving.

Making a wish is casting a spell from the heart to allow miracles to take place.

"Thank you," she whispered to the bell. Jake's change of heart was a miracle. A smile spread across her face. Frost Manor would be decorated for Christmas, even if it was for the last time. Belle's thoughts drifted. She wondered what Jake had wished for. It must have been very important for him to stop believing in miracles and magic. A part of her wanted to do something to help him move past whatever was weighing on his soul. Despite his gruff exterior, she had developed a soft spot for him. She stared at the bell's metallic surface. Since she was here, she might as well make a wish. She closed her eyes and placed her hand on the bell.

Help me find my purpose and meaning in my life again.

Belle opened one eye then closed it again.

And heal Jake's heart and help him find happiness, too.

She pushed the bell with her hand and opened her eyes. The magnificent heirloom rocked back and forth silently. Belle missed the sound of the chime. She wondered if she would ever hear its beautiful ring again.

CHAPTER 21

"Frost Manor is going to be decorated again?" Josie exclaimed. "And Jake gave you permission? It's a Christmas miracle."

"Maybe the Beast has a soft heart after all," Grayson said. He leaned forward, grabbed a handful of popcorn out of the bowl on the coffee table, and shoved it into his mouth.

Belle smiled as she sat in one of the sofas in Josie's living room. Grayson was stretched out on the adjacent couch while Josie rocked in the recliner cuddling her sleeping baby in her arms.

Josie's living room was a picture of Christmas cheer. A beautifully decorated Christmas tree stood in front of the window. Its branches were laden with twinkling lights and colorful ornaments. A plethora of wrapped gifts for baby Holly were positioned in an orderly fashion under the boughs. A crackling fireplace cast a warm glow over the room while the 1947 version of Miracle on 34th Street played on the television. The scent of pine needles, gingerbread cookies, and popcorn filled the air.

"Does that mean the Wishing Bell will be open to the public?" Grayson asked as he chomped on the popcorn.

Belle shook her head. "I can only decorate the house. The tree lot and Wishing Bell are off-limits. Apparently, he hates the Wishing Bell because it didn't grant one wish he made."

"When he was a child?" Grayson grabbed a gingerbread cookie.

Belle shrugged. "I have no idea. He wouldn't get into specifics. There's just so much about him that doesn't make sense. I feel like when I start to see who he really is, something sets him off and then he hides behind his walls again."

Josie and Grayson looked at each other from across the room. A sly smile appeared on Josie's face. "You have feelings for the Beast of Frost Manor. Don't deny it. You care a lot about Jake's wellbeing."

For once Belle didn't brush off the response. "I enjoy his company. He is handsome and he has a good heart. But I don't know how he feels about me. His mood tends to switch on and off."

"Well, he made you dinner when you two were decorating the tree," Josie said, stroking the sleeping infant's back. "Most men don't do that unless they are very interested in a woman."

"And he did save your life," added Grayson. "I know we all didn't like Jake when he first arrived, but no one would blame you if you felt something for him."

"Lately, he is growing on me. I do feel a connection when I'm around him. I kind of feel bad for him. He's all alone in that big mansion with no family around the holidays. I can almost understand why he doesn't want to celebrate. We almost kissed the other night before Jingle interrupted us. Yet I can't help but feel like there's more going on." Belle leaned back against the sofa.

"That picture in the attic is still nagging at you, isn't it?" said Josie.

Belle sighed. "I don't know who that could be. You could tell by the quality of the photo that it wasn't an old portrait. It must have been taken within the last few years. Some days I wish Sam was still here so I could talk to him about Jake. And I wish I could ask him why he is sending me on a wild goose chase to find a missing clapper."

Josie shifted the baby gently to her shoulder. Her eyes lit up. "There is someone you could ask. Pasquale Fontana."

"Who?"

"That's Sam's best friend. They've known each other for over fifty years. Sam used to have frequent meet-ups with Pasquale at the tavern to play cards and chat. He's the only person I know who could give you some insight about Jake. But I haven't seen Pasquale in months. I'll do a little digging at the bakery tomorrow and ask Shirley when she comes in. I think she's still in contact with him."

"Have you decided how you're going to decorate the mansion?" Grayson asked as he went for another cookie.

"I would like to do something to honor Sam's legacy. I've been looking at all the pictures of past Christmas displays at the manor. I'm going to do a combination," declared Belle.

"I like it. It could be a winter wonderland of Sam's creations. Christmas past and present in one place," Josie replied.

Grayson grabbed his fourth cookie. "Speaking of Sam, how goes the quest to figure out the mystery of the bell?"

"The second clue led us to an old sleigh that had another note taped underneath, but it's not like the others. It looks like a cipher or a code. Neither one of us can figure it out." Belle pulled up a picture of the notecard on her phone and placed the device on the coffee table. Her eyes focused on the numbers and letters that had been driving her crazy.

A.C.C

C.D.

19121843

Josie craned her neck to look at the photo. "Those first two rows look like initials for something. Did you try to do a web search on the numbers? Maybe it's a barcode?"

"I did that already." Belle picked up her phone and typed in the numbers. "See? All that comes up are these random websites that make no sense."

"What if we split the numbers into sections," Grayson suggested, "like a code on a padlock 19, 12, 18, 43."

"But where's the padlock?" Belle groaned.

"Are there any safes in Frost Manor?" Josie asked.

"Maybe, but I've never seen them." Belle leaned over and took a peanut butter cookie from the tray. She stared at the criss-crossed marks on the tasty morsel. "I think Jake would recognize if it was a code to one of his safes."

"Not necessarily, especially if he has a lot of safes. I always forget the code to the garage and I have to keep looking in my notes app to find it." Josie shifted her weight in the chair, careful not to wake the baby. "What if it isn't a code?" Josie raised her finger in thought. "What if it's a date? Dates follow the same pattern as the numbers on the note: Two digits for the month, two digits for the day, and four digits for the year."

"It might be." Belle raised the peanut butter cookie to her lips and took a bite.

"The date is 19-12-1843?" asked Grayson. "But there isn't a nine-teenth month."

"That's the way they write the date in Europe," Josie explained. "The month and day are switched. If the numbers are revealing a date, then it's December 19, 1843."

"1843?" Belle looked down at the partially eaten cookie in her hand. "Why would Sam use a date that occurred over a century ago? Could that be significant to Frost Manor?"

"Maybe that's when Frost Manor was built?" chimed in Grayson.

"I don't know," Josie replied. "Search it up and see what it says."

Belle placed the rest of the cookie on her plate and took her phone in her hands. After typing in the date, a list of different websites appeared with similar headings.

- *A Christmas Carol*
- *On this day in history, Charles Dickens*
- *A Christmas Carol is published*
- *History of A Christmas Carol*

"The search results are all talking about the book, *A Christmas Carol,* by Charles Dickens." Belle looked at her siblings.

"That's it!" Josie snapped her fingers. "Don't you see? The initials A.C.C. that stands for *A Christmas Carol* and C.D. is Charles Dickens."

A thrill of excitement raced through Belle. Another part of the mystery had been solved, but how many clues still remained until they reached the end?

"There are many versions of *A Christmas Carol,*" Grayson said. "Do we know which one Sam would be referencing?"

"There has to be a copy of the book at Frost Manor. Why else would Sam use it?" Josie told him.

"The mansion does have a library. I'll have to check it out tomorrow when I go." Forcing her legs to move, Belle stood up. "I should probably get going. I need to submit my resume to a few more places."

"Any job interviews?" Greyson stood and stretched his arms over his head.

"No."

"You're still looking for a job in New York City?" Josie asked.

"The agency I'm working with said that because of the upcoming holiday, it might take longer than expected. And yes, Josie, I'm looking for a job in the city. That's my home." Belle picked up the empty paper plates, walked over to the kitchen, and dumped them into the garbage.

"Falls Village is also your home and it's where your family is. It's been so nice to see you every day instead of just on holidays. Your nieces and nephews miss you all the time. If you stayed, you could watch them grow up. Maybe you could even spend more time with Jake, too." Josie winked at her and continued to rock Holly in her arms. "You're such a great artist. You could open your own gallery here and then create more of your masterpieces for everyone to enjoy." She nodded to the painting on the mantle.

Belle smiled. "I understand what you're trying to do, but if a gallery in New York City was having a hard time keeping the doors open, I don't think people in Falls Village would be interested either. Besides, I worked for a decade in the city. I can't let all my hard work and education go to waste."

"I think people here in Vermont would be interested in your paintings," replied Josie.

After hugging her siblings goodbye, Belle stepped out into the chilly night air. A sense of confusion washed over her. New York was her home, but she couldn't deny it was nice being back with family. There was something about the country air that made her feel refreshed and calm. As she got into her car and started the engine, she hoped the Wishing Bell would work its magic soon.

CHAPTER 22

"Why won't anyone give me a chance?" muttered Belle as she hit the submit button on her laptop. She must have submitted over twenty applications in the last few hours to different companies in the Big Apple. A ding on her laptop announced she had received an email. Clicking on the message, Belle saw it was from her headhunter.

I found a job that may be a good fit for you. I'll be in touch soon.

Leaning her head back against the array of pillows sprawled across her bed, Belle sighed. Her laptop rested on her thighs, the email staring back at her. The unknown weighed heavily on her soul. While she was grateful she had been able to save a lot of money over the years, she couldn't be without a job forever.

The only people benefitting from her series of unfortunate events were her parents. They were absolutely delighted to have her back home. Even though they told her she could stay as long as she liked, Belle yearned for her own place again.

Closing the laptop, Belle placed it on her nightstand. The clock read midnight. She should be asleep by now, but instead, she was wide awake. Stress pumped through her, making her uneasy and on edge. Sliding off the bed, she walked over to the window and pulled back the curtains. She peered through the blinds at the winter wonderland that covered the farm. A light flurry fell peacefully onto the ground and trees. White flakes were highlighted against the dark sky by the spotlights. Not far from the house were the two barns that housed the animals.

Belle's eyes focused on the upper part of the second barn, particularly the lone window on the left side. Through that window was a memory of a happier time in Belle's life. A place where she could be herself and do what she loved best. Curiosity took hold of her and Belle left her room. Silence greeted her as she headed downstairs. Everyone else in the house was deep in slumber while she walked around like the night watchman. She took her heavy winter coat out of the closet and put it on over her pajamas. Then she wrapped her scarf around her neck, slid on a pair of boots, and pulled a knitted cap over her head. Belle opened the back door and entered into the chilly night air. The snow was deep as she trudged across the yard toward the barns.

Snowflakes fell around her, kissing her hair and cheeks. The tiny flakes landed on her blue coat, leaving miniscule droplets of water in their wake. Wrapping her fingers around the handle to the second barn, Belle pulled the door open. Flicking on the light, she looked down the aisle and saw some of the horses stick their heads out.

"I'm sorry to wake you all," Belle apologized as she walked down the corridor. The horses snorted and nickered. Belle rubbed her gloved hands over their muzzles and scratched behind their ears.

At the back of the barn was a wooden staircase. The steps creaked under her weight, but Belle knew they had been built sturdy by her uncle. A feeling of nostalgia washed over her as she climbed higher and higher. At the top of the stairs was a door with a sign that read: Belle's Art Studio. Opening the door, a circular rug caught her attention. The pine tree pattern that wove around the knotted edge had been handmade by her grandmother. Brushes and paint covered the nearby shelves and easels were scattered about the room. Some were covered in dust sheets while others were bare and ready for inspiration. Paintings decorated the walls.

Her paintings.

A tinge of sadness tugged at her heart. It had been a long time since she had stood in the place that her family had created for her. Walking further into the room, Belle ran her fingers along the empty canvases and easels. In the center of the room was a stand with a dust covering and a little chair in front. This was where she used to sit and paint for hours. She never wanted to leave. Wrapping her fingers around the sheet, Belle pulled her arm back and was greeted with a half-finished painting of her parents' house.

When did I paint this? And why didn't I finish it?

Questions bounced around in her head as she sat down in the chair. She glanced at the stand next to her where a container of brushes stood. Folding her hands, she narrowed her eyes at the dried, crusted tips stained with paint. A memory that had been buried for years resurfaced, filling her heart with a forgotten pain. Tears pricked at the corners of her eyes, and the bitter taste of failure danced on her tongue. Glancing around the room one final time, Belle stood up and left.

CHAPTER 23

"If I was *A Christmas Carol,* where would I hide?" Belle placed her hands on her hips and scanned the shelves of the library at Frost Manor. She had been staring at the spines for the past forty-five minutes, but the book she needed wasn't there.

Belle took a minute to admire the extravagant room. After the solarium, this was her second favorite place in the mansion. The high ceilings were adorned with intricate plasterwork. Mahogany and walnut bookcases stretched from the floor to the ceiling and were decorated with fancy carvings. Rows of leather-bound books covered the shelves. Their spines were etched with fancy gold lettering. A large bay window was framed by heavy velvet drapes, and a seat had been built into the recess beneath the frame. The window seat was upholstered in damask, and the plump cushions invited her to rest and read. A marble fireplace was framed by plush armchairs and velvet chaise lounges. Persian rugs covered the floors, and a large crystal chandelier hung overhead. Side tables were decorated with globes and telescopes. The scent of old paper filled her nostrils.

Belle could hear Jake's voice floating into the room from his office, where he was taking part in a virtual meeting. She knew she had to get started on the decorations if she was going to have the place ready for Christmas. Leaving the sanctuary of knowledge, Belle walked down the hall into the living room, where the beautiful Christmas tree glittered before her. A smile crossed her face as her thoughts drifted to the other night. It had been a long time since she had done something festive with a man, and it felt nice. Nails clicked on the wood floor behind her. Jingle appeared at her side, his pink tongue dangling.

"Hey, buddy." Belle knelt next to the massive Saint Bernard and rubbed her fingers through his fur. "You wouldn't happen to know where *A Christmas Carol* is hidden, would you?" In response, Jingle lumbered off to his dog bed in front of the fire. He crawled onto the red cushion and laid down. "I didn't think so." Belle flopped onto the couch and grabbed the thick binder Jake had left for her. Phone numbers, business cards, and newspaper clippings met her eyes as she flipped through the pages. Belle had already decided that she would need professionals for the exterior and interior of the mansion. But she felt differently about the living room. This was the place she and Jake had bonded over the Christmas tree, and she wanted to finish decorating the space herself.

Closing the binder, Belle walked over to the closet near the solarium. Covering the living room in holiday cheer would be her first task of the day. Belle carried the lighter boxes and dragged the heavier ones into the living room. Once she was done, she pulled out her phone and pressed play on her Christmas playlist. Seasonal tunes filled the room as Belle took strings of lights and set to work transforming the space into a Christmas masterpiece.

She draped garlands covered with red berries and pine cones along the fireplace. On the mantle, she placed snowmen, candles, and little Christmas figurines around the portrait of the Frost couple. On either side of the hearth, she placed two large poinsettia plants. Ornate candles in gold holders were situated in the window sill. She hung portraits of winter scenes and wreaths on the wall. Holiday pillows and burgundy throws accented the sofas and armchairs. At the bottom of one of the boxes, she found velvet stockings embroidered with the Frost family's initials, which she hung from the mantel.

Belle wiped her sweaty hands on her joggers as she looked around at her hard work. "One room down, only a hundred or so to go." She turned to Jingle who barked in approval.

Her next task was to get the other Christmas boxes from the attic and basement and bring them into the sunroom. After another hour of hard labor, Belle accomplished the task. She sat on one of the chests to catch her breath.

"The living room is stunning," Jake's voice boomed. He appeared in the doorframe with his hands in the pockets of his slacks. "You did an outstanding job."

"Thank you." Belle gave him a grin as she wiped the back of her hand across her sweaty forehead.

"You brought all those boxes up yourself?" Jake glanced at the assortment of storage containers.

"They were pretty light. That's probably why there are so many," replied Belle. "I'm going to hire professionals to decorate the rest of the manor. This is a lot of work." She glanced at the messy pile of boxes and crates. "Wait a minute. I forgot a box. The one that has the Christmas Village in it."

"Where is it?" Jake asked.

"It's in the attic. It's a small brown box at the back of the attic, near the old desk."

"I'll go get it," he told her. "You worked really hard this morning. Take a rest and drink some water."

"Thank you." Belle walked into the living room and sank into the sofa.

She heard Jake's leather shoes clacking against the wood floors as he headed to the attic. Jingle padded over and placed his head in Belle's lap. She scratched the back of his ears as her mind drifted to where the book could be hidden.

I'll ask Jake when he returns.

A few minutes passed, and Jake still hadn't come back.

What is taking him so long? Maybe I should go check on him.

Belle placed her hand on the armrest to get up when Jake appeared. His hands clutched the sides of the box so tight his knuckles were white. A scowl was etched across his face. His eyebrows were low and his eyes were dark. He placed the box down on the floor in front of Belle.

"Thank you..." Belle's voice trailed off as he turned on his heel and walked away. "Where are you going?"

Jake didn't respond and continued down the hallway.

"Jake." Belle got up from the sofa and walked out into the hallway, but he had disappeared. She turned to Jingle who stood next to her. "What's his problem?" The Saint Bernard gave a whimper and lumbered off to the kitchen. "Where did he go?" Belle wandered down the east hall. At the end of the corridor were two elegant white doors etched in a gold leaf pattern.

"I've never been to this side of the house," she murmured. "What's behind these doors?"

She put both hands on the white-painted wood, pushing through into an unknown room. Belle's jaw dropped as she stepped into a massive ballroom.

An inlaid wood floor stretched before her. Palladian windows surrounded the space, spilling in light from every angle. Three giant crystal chandeliers hung from the ceiling and marble columns spanned the area. Tiny etchings of gold leaves decorated the white walls, and a brick fireplace was on the far side of the room.

Belle turned in circles as her footsteps echoed throughout the room. She felt like she had stepped into a royal Christmas movie where she was a beautiful princess about to dance with a handsome prince. Her daydream was interrupted by Jingle barking. Belle saw the Saint Bernard standing in the entranceway. His jowls swung back and forth as a rapid set of barks escaped his mouth.

"What is it, boy?" Belle asked him.

Jingle turned and lumbered down the hall like a small bear. Belle followed the canine as he led her to the solarium. He scratched at the closed entrance and whimpered.

"What's wrong, buddy?" Belle pressed on the handle and secretly hoped that Jake was inside. She wanted to make sure he was alright.

The silence of the roses and plants greeted them as they entered. Jingle trotted across the room and jumped up onto the window seat near the glass. He laid on the cream-colored cushions and began basking in the sunlight.

"You wanted the warm sun, didn't you?" Belle grabbed a watering can and stepped into the small room off of the solarium. She filled the watering can in the sink. Gardening tools and bags of fertilizer lined the shelves. Stepping back into the solarium, she watered a few of the rose bushes. The mysterious black rose caught her attention.

Belle glared at the petals and restrained the urge to throw the flower into the garbage. Its deathly ambience cast a gloomy vibe over the colorful room.

Why is Jake keeping that rose in here? As soon as I find him, I'm going to ask him.

Underneath the vase that held the rose were three leather-bound books with decorations and notches on the spine. Belle moved closer so she could read the gold lettering.

Jane Eyre
Pride and Prejudice
A Christmas Carol

Belle almost dropped the watering can. The book she had been looking for had been in front of her face the whole time. Rushing forward, Belle removed the vase from on top of the books and placed it on the glass table. Settling onto the garden sofa, Belle flipped through the book, letting the pages rush in a blur before her. She checked the inside and outside cover, but there wasn't a clue.

How is that possible? This can't be the last task. I must be missing something.

Putting back the watering can, Belle decided to borrow the book and look at it more carefully after a hot shower. The Grandfather clock in the hall chimed three. It was time for her to leave. She had promised Josie she would oversee the bakery for the rest of the afternoon. Heading back into the main part of the house, Belle grabbed her purse and Sam's binder.

"Jake," Belle called. "Jake, where are you?"

There was no response. Belle didn't have time to continue searching for him. Pulling out her phone, she typed out a text: Hi Jake. I'm leaving to go help at the bakery. I'll be back tomorrow. I hope you're alright."

Jingle appeared at her side, whimpering. She looked at the Saint Bernard. "Let's make sure you're fed before I leave."

Walking into the kitchen, she took the canine's food out of the cabinet. She poured the rest of it into his dish and walked over to throw the empty bag in the trash. When she looked down, she noticed that the garbage can was filled to the top.

I'll empty it. I'm leaving anyway.

Belle tied up the garbage and dragged the trash out of the house to the waste containers. She threw back the lid, and was about to hurl the garbage inside when something caught her eye. On top of the array of white bags was the portrait of the woman Belle had found in the attic. The photo was in bad shape. More chunks of glass had fallen out of the frame, and the picture had been scratched as if someone had clawed their nails across the image.

Who is this woman? Jake must have found the portrait in the attic and threw it in the trash. But why? Belle took the photo.

What are you doing, Belle? Leave the photo -- it's none of your business, her thoughts lectured her. However, Belle couldn't let it go. Perhaps this woman was responsible for Jake's hatred of Christmas. If she figured out the connection, maybe she could help Jake heal and love the holidays again. Looking around to make sure no one was watching her, Belle raced over to her car and stashed the picture in her glove box. Then she went back inside the manor, got the rest of her things, and left.

CHAPTER 24

Morning rays of sun warmed Belle's face as she sat on the porch at Frost Manor. Today was the day the decorators would transform the mansion into the epitome of seasonal elegance. The rumble of an engine caught her attention as an emerald green sports car entered the driveway and pulled up in front of the manor.

Belle walked down the steps to greet the guest. An older woman in her fifties stepped out of the small car. She wore a red tailored suit with a Christmas tree pin on the lapel. Red-bottom shoes and ruby nails completed her outfit. The winter wind whipped the woman's blonde hair across her face. She moved her hands to gain control of her locks, then turned to Belle. "Belle Winters?"

"That's me." Belle extended her hand.

"Evelyn Twinkle." The woman interlocked her hand with Belle's and shook it. "I'm so happy you decided to go with our company, Christmas Sisters, for your decor."

"I couldn't have done it by myself," Belle answered.

Evelyn stepped back and sized up the mansion. "It's an honor to be able to decorate this house. Sam did an exquisite job all those years. I'm touched you chose us to honor his memory." She rummaged through her bag and pulled out a clipboard. "I'm going to make some notes for our consultation. I want to be able to tailor everything to your vision. Will your husband be joining us?"

"What? No...I...," Belle tried to correct Evelyn's assumption, but the decorator kept on chatting.

"How many square feet is Frost Manor?" Evelyn asked, raising her pen.

"Fifteen thousand, five hundred."

Evelyn shrugged. "Piece of cake. I've decorated entire malls before. This place always reminded me of a castle. As I stated over the phone, I'll be in charge of decorating the exterior of Frost Manor. My twin sister Ivy will be in charge of the interior. She'll meet with you this afternoon."

"I look forward to working with her." Belle replied as they began to walk the perimeter of the house.

"Magnificent!" Evelyn scribbled notes on her clipboard. "But I must say, it's a bit late to be starting the decorum. Never fear. We'll get it done on time. This is why my sisters and I started Christmas Sisters Decorating. We wanted to help everyone be able to decorate their homes in a timely manner and not have to worry about breaking the bank." Evelyn stopped at the fountain. "Oh, this is lovely. We can decorate it with some pinecones, evergreens, and poinsettias. And these bushes that run along the front of the house, we can weave lights through them."

As Evelyn continued to gush about her vision for Frost Manor, Belle's thoughts drifted to Jake. Where was he? This morning she had arrived late and hadn't had time to check on him.

"Where are my manners? What is your vision for Frost Manor, Belle?" Evelyn's voice brought Belle back to reality.

"I have a few ideas. We want to honor the former owners, Sam and Agnes Frost." Belle pulled her phone from her pocket and went to her photos. She showed Evelyn the images from newspaper articles and magazines that had featured Frost Manor.

"Combining the past with the present. I love it." Evelyn jotted down more notes. "When you have a chance later, email me those photos. I'll come up with a proposal according to your requests."

The two women walked along the side of the house as Evelyn continued her evaluation. "We can line the roof in lights and put wreaths over the garages and front door." Evelyn tapped her pen against her cheek.

"I would like to see candles in all the windows, too," Belle added. "Sam did that each year. He always said the candles were the light of Jesus, giving people hope during the holidays."

"Of course. More lights and more wreaths. We can also put pine boughs over the outside lamps." Evelyn made more scribbles in her notebook.

"We have a lot of the outside decor pieces stored in the garage and the equipment barn," added Belle.

"Excellent. It's always easier for us when customers have their own decorations. Most companies and homes finished decorating last month, so you will have our undivided attention."

They walked into the backyard. Evelyn gushed over how grand the back porch looked and made notes about needing more garland for the columns and railings. Belle stared into the distance at the horses grazing in the pasture. Two Clydesdales, an Appaloosa, and a Quarter Horse roamed around. Some had their heads bowed searching for sprigs of grass, while others trotted around, engaging in playful chases. A figure leaned against the fence watching the horses. Belle's heart skipped a beat.

It was Jake.

A happiness surrounded Belle as she stared at the Beast of Frost Manor. Then the image of the woman pierced her thoughts, instantly chilling her mood. The portrait was still sitting in the glove compartment of her car. How could she bring it up to Jake without making it seem like she was meddling? After all, the picture had been dumped into the garbage for a reason.

"Do you want to decorate the barns too?" Evelyn asked. "I think it would really add to the overall ambiance."

"Maybe we should stick to the house for now. We're only a few weeks away from Christmas," Belle answered, turning her eyes away from Jake.

"True, true."

"How long do you think it will take to decorate the manor?" Belle asked.

"I employ a lot of people, so probably a day. Two days, max." Evelyn looked up from her clipboard and saw Jake in the distance. "Oh my, your husband is so handsome."

Belle felt heat rise to her cheeks, and she was sure her face was as crimson as Evelyn's outfit. "He isn't my husband. Jake is the owner of Frost Manor. We're friends, and he's having me decorate the place due to his busy schedule."

"Well, if I were about twenty years younger and single, I would be asking him out." Evelyn placed her hand on Belle's shoulder and chuckled. "You two would make a good couple. I know it's none of my business. But you young folks tend to be so focused on your careers and making a name for yourself that you forget about the most important part of life: having someone to share it with. Love is a beautiful thing, especially at Christmas. My Harry and I were wed on Christmas Eve. It was magical. But I'm sure you don't want to hear an old lady reminisce. I'll take the photos you sent me and I'll come up with a blueprint for Frost Manor. Then, you can let me know if we need to change or add anything. I should have that for you tonight."

"Thank you so much for seeing me on such short notice." Belle said as they walked back to Evelyn's car.

"The pleasure is all mine." Evelyn placed her clipboard into her leather bag. "I'm excited to work with you. Ivy said she'll be over around two o'clock for a consultation about the interior."

"I'll be here," Belle assured her.

"Wonderful. I'll be in touch." Evelyn got into her car.

Belle waved goodbye as the business woman drove off. Then she walked back to the pastures. Jake still hadn't moved from his earlier position. He leaned against the fence with his foot on the lowest rail. His forearms rested on the upper railing and his chin was on his hands.

Jingle came bounding out of one of the barns and trotted across the snow-covered grass. He stopped beside Belle, his tail wagging.

"Hi, boy," she said as she stroked his head.

Jingle turned and took off across the yard and Belle walked over to Jake.

"Penny for your thoughts?" she asked as she leaned against the railing next to him.

Jake raised his head abruptly and turned in the direction of her voice. "Belle, when did you get here?"

"About forty-five minutes ago. Are you alright?"

"Yes, I'm fine." Jake rested his fingers against his temples for a moment. "I have a lot on my mind. I've been working all hours of the night lately, and I can't seem to get enough sleep."

"You need to take some time for yourself." Belle replied as she watched the horses roaming around. "Christmas is the time to slow down and enjoy life."

"Christmas is the time I try to stay the busiest. That way, it'll come and go as quickly as possible."

"Yes, that's right. I forgot you're a Christmas hater," Belle teased.

Jake furrowed his brow and looked at her. "I don't hate Christmas."

Belle couldn't hold back the giggle that escaped her lips. "Of course not. Everyone turns into a stubborn, angry person whenever the word Christmas is mentioned."

"I decorated a tree with you, didn't I?" He rolled his eyes.

"Yes. After I bothered you for weeks about it."

"I could say the same about you. Why do you hate painting?" He turned to look at her, holding her attention with his emerald gaze.

Belle's face was a mixture of shock and bewilderment. She hadn't expected Jake to turn the conversation around on her. Her mouth parted and she managed to get out the words, "I don't hate painting."

"Then why did you stop? I've been staring at that painting in the office for the past eleven months, wondering who the artist was. Then she shows up at my door in a bundle of holiday charm, and she doesn't paint anymore." Jake's gaze pressured her to address the feelings she wanted to lock away forever.

"You seem to be the only one who thinks my paintings are beautiful," Belle muttered. She looked down at the rough edges of the rails.

"What does that even mean?" Jake moved closer to her. "I highly doubt that. Your family and your friends love your paintings. They have them displayed all over their houses and in their businesses."

Belle continued to stare at the fence. She took a deep breath. "It was the summer before I went to college. I was seventeen and I submitted one of my paintings to a prestigious art show in Montpelier. I was so excited and I really thought they would pick me. Then the letter came saying that my painting didn't fit the direction they were going in, and it wouldn't be accepted into the gallery. If they'd left it at that, I would have been fine. But the curator continued to say how my work was amateur at best, and I'd be better off taking a different career path."

"They said that to you?" Jake's eyes widened.

Belle nodded.

"I'm sorry, Belle." Jake placed his hand over hers.

Tears pricked at the corners of Belle's eyes. "I was devastated. I spent hours working on that painting. Their criticism made me wonder if I was even good enough to be an artist. I didn't want to submit my work to that art gallery in the first place, but my family convinced me. Even Sam encouraged me. Then, to hear those experts say I wasn't good enough, it made me feel like all the compliments I received from my friends and family were fake." Belle paused. "The painting I submitted was the portrait of Frost Manor. When I got the rejection letter, I wanted to throw the painting into the garbage. Sam convinced me not to and said he would take my painting. I gave it to him and it's been in Frost Manor ever since."

Jake smiled. "I'm grateful my grandfather persuaded you to give it to him. Now I get to enjoy your talent every day at the office. Don't listen to what those people say. It's only one art gallery. There are hundreds of art galleries in the United States. For every person who doesn't like your work, there are thousands who will. You can't give up on your talent Belle. I hope you find it in your heart to paint again. I would love to see more of your work." Jake removed his hand from on top of hers. He shifted his position so his back was against the fence and his hands were shoved in his pockets. "It's crazy. My grandfather was the Christmas King of Falls Village, and here I am, a Beast and a Scrooge. I used to love Christmas until it became a painful reminder of the most horrible time in my life."

"What happened?" Belle asked cautiously.

He cleared his throat. "I appreciate you telling me how you feel, Belle. In return, I will tell you some of my story, just not right now. Have you figured out the next part of the mystery?

Belle held back a groan. She hated when he clammed up like a turtle hiding in its shell. How much longer would she have to wait to find the truth? She sighed. "My sister and brother helped me discover the answer. It's the book, *A Christmas Carol*."

"That's one of my favorite novels." Jake ran his gloved hand along the top of the fence.

Well, that's no surprise, given your humbug attitude. Belle chided herself for being so inconsiderate. "I found the book in the solarium."

"That's right. I used that book and the other ones as a stand for my rose."

"But that book is a first edition," Belle pointed out. "Shouldn't it be locked up? Those books are worth thousands of dollars."

Jake shrugged. "I suppose you're right. But no one comes here anyway. I'm the Beast, remember? The last time I glanced at that novel, I didn't see anything that would stand out as a clue. Are you sure?"

"I'm positive. It fits with the Christmas theme. Bell, sleigh, book. They're all related to each other. I checked the book too and I didn't see any clues," noted Belle.

Jake peeled himself from the fence. "I can take another look at it." He started walking toward the house.

"It's in my bag. I borrowed it for the night." Belle followed him.

"How did the meeting with the decorating company go?" Jake raised his voice over the December wind that whipped around them.

"It went well. I met with the exterior designer and later this afternoon, the interior designer will be over," replied Belle.

"You were right, by the way. It was a good idea to decorate the manor to honor Grandpa. He would have wanted me to continue his legacy. I'm sorry I couldn't see that earlier. I wish there was something more I could do to honor my grandfather."

"What about opening up the Christmas tree lot and bringing back the Wishing Bell?" Belle hinted. She hoped his grinchy spirit wouldn't obstruct her creative flow.

"We're going to ask people to make wishes on a bell that doesn't ring?" Jake raised his eyebrows.

Belle slumped her shoulders. "You're right. I forgot about that. Are you sure you didn't sabotage it?"

"Me?" Jake placed a hand on his chest. "Do you have any idea how heavy that clapper is? Look at the size of the bell. What would I even do with it? No, I didn't take it. I'm sure my grandfather is the one who took the clapper for this treasure hunt of his."

Their boots crunched in the snow as they walked back to the mansion.

"Opening the Christmas tree lot this year wouldn't be profitable. Most families have already gotten their trees and there isn't enough time for me to hire people to work the lots."

"I guess you're right." Belle walked up the back steps.

"Maybe we could try for next year." Jake saw the look on Belle's face. "Don't hold me to it. I said maybe." Jake opened the kitchen door, letting her enter first.

Belle bit back a smile. Could the Christmas spirit finally be working its way into Jake's heart? She took the book out of her bag and gave it to Jake. Then they walked to the solarium.

"I don't know what it is about this room, but I always feel calmer when I'm in here," Belle said as they were enveloped by the intoxicating perfume of roses.

"Grandpa used to say the same thing." Jake sat down on the garden sofa and ran his fingers over the brown-ribbed cloth cover of the book. "The green endpapers inside are what signifies it is a first edition. Grandpa always loved his rare books." Using his thumb, he let the pages fall one after another in a rapid motion. "I don't see any notes hidden in the pages." He glanced at the endpapers. "There don't appear to be any codes printed." Jake shook his head and snapped the book shut. "That note must have meant something else."

Belle shook her head. Her eyes fell on the black rose and she couldn't contain herself any longer. "Jake. Why do you have a black rose?"

Jake turned to her. "What?"

Belle pointed to the vase.

Taking the rose, Jake held the flower up to the light and twirled it between his thumb and index finger. "Black roses don't exist in nature. I dyed the petals that color."

"Why?"

"To serve as a painful reminder of something I will never do." He placed the rose back into the vase. "This rose symbolizes my choice to never fall in love again."

CHAPTER 25

*T*his black rose symbolizes my choice to never fall in love again. Jake's surprising confession echoed in Belle's mind as she pulled up to her family's ranch in the late afternoon.

"That's an extreme case of heartbreak to dye a rose black," Belle murmured as she turned off her car, grabbed her bag, and walked to the house.

When she had asked Jake what had happened to make him feel that way, he brushed her off. The news was disappointing. Over the past few weeks, she had grown fond of Jake. She thought he felt the same way but maybe it had been her imagination. After his latest declaration, it was clear he wasn't looking for love anytime soon.

Belle took a walk around the property. She watched the farm animals in the pasture enjoying the brisk air. Her eyes fell on the loft window of the second barn.

Why do you hate painting? I don't understand why you stopped. Jake's words from their earlier conversation played in her memory.

I don't hate painting. There just wasn't any time when I went to college, and then I went to work in the city. Her heart sank as she gripped the top railing of the pasture and looked at the cows. *I could have made time. I could have tried. But I was scared of not being good enough.*

Turning away from the grazing cows, Belle walked by a flock of chickens that pecked and scratched at the dirt. She entered the second barn, passed the empty stalls, and headed up the wooden staircase. She stepped into her art studio and placed her purse on the nearby chair. Taking off her coat and hanging it on the wall hook, Belle rolled up her sleeves and grabbed a clean smock off the hanger. With shaking hands, Belle removed the dust sheet from the covered painting to reveal the portrait of her parents' half-painted house.

"I don't hate painting," she muttered as she pulled her long hair into a ponytail. In the nearby cabinets, she found brand-new bottles of paint instead of dried-up containers with caked color on the lids.

"What is this?" She peered further into the cabinets to find new paintbrushes along with more jars of acrylic, oil, and water-color paints. A smile crossed her face. Her family was behind the new art supplies. They had never given up on her talent.

Bringing her tools to the table, Belle picked up a paintbrush and stared at the painting. A surge of courage had pushed her to the easel. She would no longer fear failure. The canvas had been a daunting void that had intimidated her for too long. Her hand trembled as she dipped the brush into a vibrant pool of turquoise. Her first stroke was hesitant as the color moved across the canvas. But as the paint flowed, something within her ignited. She had forgotten the excitement that came with painting and the power to create her own interpretation of the world.

As vibrant colors danced across the canvas, her strokes grew bolder and more confident. The snowy world outside the loft faded away as she lost herself in the rhythm of creation. With each brushstroke, a weight lifted from her shoulders. The portrait was no longer filled with blank spaces, but a world that blossomed with joy, hope, and sorrow. It was a raw, unfiltered expression of her soul that filled her with a sensation she hadn't felt in years. She didn't know how many hours had passed and she didn't care. Placing her brush in the holder, Belle took a step back and admired her work. Tears of joy welled in her eyes. The canvas was an old friend, welcoming her back with open arms. She had returned to doing what she loved best.

A creak from a foot on the stairs sounded behind her.

"Honey, are you up here?" her father's voice called to her.

"Yes, Dad, I am." Belle turned to see her father enter the studio. He brought with him the scent of fresh Vermont air and her mom's gingerbread cookies.

"I was wondering where you had gone." He ran his fingers through his white hair. "I thought you might be out playing with the animals, but secretly I was hoping you'd be here. Turns out I was right."

Belle laughed. "You knew I'd end up back here eventually."

"A true artist may need a break from time to time, but the painter in her never leaves. It's good to see you back in your element." Her father's boots clunked on the wooden boards as he walked closer. He let out a low whistle as he laid eyes on her painting. "Look at that masterpiece. I knew you would finish it. Wow." He beamed with pride at the completed painting of Winters' Farm.

"I'm thinking of giving it to Mom as a Christmas gift," said Belle.

"She'll love it." Her father placed his arm around her shoulders. "I already do."

"Did you buy me new art supplies?"

"We all did. When you told us you were coming home, we decided to fix this place up. When you were a little girl, this was the place you would always go to when you were upset. Painting is in your blood."

"You're right. I feel calmer. I don't even know why I stopped painting to begin with."

"You know why you stopped." Her father pulled up a chair and gestured for her to sit down. "Rejection will do that to you. It will make you second guess yourself, and make you feel like you're not good enough. But if you base your life on people's acceptance, you'll find yourself miserable and unhappy. Instead of retreating into the deepest parts of your fears, take the rejection and use it to propel yourself forward. As you grow, you learn, and become a better version of yourself."

Belle felt her eyes grow wet. "You're right, dad."

"And remember, don't ever let anyone who isn't paying your bills or fighting your battles tell you how to live your life. Sometimes we get off track and things don't go the way we planned, but in the end it all works out. Just like I knew you would find your way back to painting. Maybe this time, instead of working for an art gallery, you'll create your own." He cleared his throat and rose to his feet. "Now, your mom wanted me to tell you that dinner is ready. Are you coming?"

Belle glanced out the window to see darkness had descended on Falls Village. "I'll be there in a minute."

Her father leaned forward and kissed the top of her head. "I'm proud of you, honey. I know your future looks confusing for the moment, but you'll find where you belong."

Belle stared at the painting as she listened to her father's boots thump down the stairs. It felt good to paint again. Picking up her paintbrushes, she brought them over to the sink and rinsed them. Her mood was different. Even though the dark cloud of unemployment still loomed over her head, her soul felt lighter. She was happy.

Hanging her smock up on the wall, Belle grabbed her phone and unlocked it. She wanted to take a picture of her painting and send it to her siblings. After snapping the picture, she opened the photo app. As she stared at the image, her finger slipped to the right. The portrait of Sam and Agnes Frost at the Christmas Gala appeared on her screen. Belle looked at the couple dressed in their elegant attire. Their arms were linked together and they were laughing. The joy on their faces warmed Belle's heart. She placed a finger on Agnes' beautiful red dress and Sam's crimson three-piece suit. An idea popped into her head. There was another way for Jake to honor their memory and prove to Falls Village he wasn't a beast after all.

CHAPTER 26

"Jake," Belle called as she entered Frost Manor. The door had been left unlocked. "Jake!" Her soul was light and happiness swirled around her. She felt accomplished after finishing the painting. Tonight, she planned to start on a new portrait and she couldn't wait. A bark greeted her instead of Jake's voice. Jingle trotted into the room. His tail wagged. Belle placed her hand on his head and scratched behind his ear.

"Hey, handsome. Where's Jake?"

Jingle barked again and turned around. He trotted over to the kitchen door and looked back at Belle.

"He's outside?" She opened the door. Jingle bolted across the snow. Belle followed. In the distance, Belle saw Jake by the Wishing Bell. As he stared at the large decorative heirloom, next to him was a sheep on a leash.

"Jake!"

Jake raised his head as Belle came closer.

"Good morning, Belle."

Belle grabbed his arm. "I painted last night." Outside of her family, Jake had been the first person she had wanted to tell about restarting her hobby.

A smile broke across Jake's face. Taking his free arm, he

wrapped her in a hug. "Yes! I knew you would paint again. I'm so proud of you."

Belle released herself from the hug and stepped back. She stared at the harness that was fastened around the sheep's body. "Why do you have a sheep on a leash?"

Jake laughed. "This is Gingerbread. She has a bad habit of escaping from her pen and wandering about the yard. This morning while I was making my coffee, I found her staring at me through the kitchen door. I just finished fixing her pen and thought we'd take a stroll around the property."

Belle knelt down and placed her gloved hand on the sheep's head. "Her coat is so fluffy."

"I like animals better than people." Jake reached down and stroked the sheep's nose. "Animals love unconditionally and don't expect anything in return." He paused for a moment. "But I must admit, I do enjoy spending time with you, Belle."

"I like spending time with you, too." Belle stood and the two stared at each other for a moment. Belle felt her cheeks grow hot.

Jake walked toward the barn with Gingerbread at his side. "When I was young, my grandparents always told me that Christmas was a magical time of year, where anything was possible. It was a time to help others and appreciate the little things. Grandpa always said there was nothing better than love at Christmas. I thought the same for a long time until I didn't."

"What changed?" Belle asked.

"Life changed me. People changed me. The world is cruel. Many times you think you know someone and then after a while you realize they were wearing a mask. You find out you were being used and the love you fought so hard for was never real." Jake stopped and stared at the bell. He touched the wooden yoke. "That's why I gave up on wishes. You can wish for people to change their ways. You can wish for them to love you. You can wish all you want but in the end it never comes true. But enough of my rambling. When are the decorators coming?"

"Tomorrow." Belle replied. Each day Jake seemed to be

opening up to her more but he still wasn't elaborating on his troubles. She would have to be patient with him. "I wanted to tell you that I thought of another way to honor your grandparents' legacy. If you're interested."

"I'm interested. What do you suggest?" Jake looked at her.

"Let's hold the Christmas Gala at Frost Manor."

Shock covered Jake's face. "You can't be serious. At Frost Manor? Where would we fit everyone?"

"In the ballroom in the East Wing, of course. I stumbled on the space yesterday and the idea came to me." Belle grabbed her phone and showed Jake the image of Sam and Agnes. "Hear me out. Look at this picture of your grandparents dressed for the gala. See how happy they are? We could call it the Frost Christmas Gala in honor of Sam and Agnes. All of the proceeds from the ticket sales can go to helping families in need during the holidays. I'm sure everyone in town would love a night where they could get dressed up and have fun."

"I'm supposed to plan an entire gala in less than two weeks?" Intrigue lined Jake's face.

"You don't have to do anything. I have it all covered. I spent all night thinking about it. My sister-in-law's friend owns a catering company. My sister's bakery will make the desserts. We don't have to worry about decorations because we already have the company doing that. To get the word out, we can post about it on all the social media platforms and pass out flyers. We can host it on December Twenty-Third in the beautifully decorated ballroom. It will be a great way to help the town get to know you and see a different side of you."

Jake knelt down and stroked Gingerbread's head, taking in everything she said. He stood up. "Fine. Go ahead. Knock yourself out."

Belle squealed and wrapped her arms around his neck. "Thank you. Thank you."

Jake dropped the leash and Gingerbread moseyed over to a

patch of grass. His muscular arms circled Belle's waist, pulling her closer to him. His face rested against her hair and Belle felt comfortable in his embrace. A sadness washed through her as she remembered how Jake had sworn off love. She wished he would give love a chance.

"It's been a while since I had a hug like this," Jake said.

Belle stepped back and smiled. "Me too." She looked back at the manor. "I'm going to head inside and start planning the gala."

"I'm going to take Gingerbread back to her stall," Jake headed to the barn.

As Belle walked to the house, she glanced over her shoulder and watched Jake. Her phone vibrated in her pocket. Pulling out her device, she saw the familiar New York number for Snowden's Recruiting Agency.

"Hello?"

"Good morning, Belle. It's Aubrey."

"Hi, Aubrey. How are you doing?" Belle opened the back door and stepped into the kitchen. She sandwiched her phone between her ear and her shoulder as she pulled off her gloves.

"I'm good. How are you doing?"

"I'm surviving," Belle said as she wiped her feet on the mat.

"I think I can change your mood. I have good news. I was able to snag you an interview with The Chenello Museum of Art. They're looking for a director of marketing."

"The Chenello," Belle gasped. "That's one of the most prestigious art galleries in New York City."

"Yes, it is, and I really talked up your expertise in the art world. Would you be available for an interview on Thursday?" Aubrey asked.

"In New York City? I'm still in Vermont." Belle walked into the kitchen and leaned on the counter.

"Yes. I told them you're on vacation. They want to do a video interview."

"That will work." Belle made a note in her calendar app.

"Perfect. I'll send all of the details and the links for the video chat to your email."

"Thank you so much." Belle disconnected the call. She placed her device on the granite then ran her fingers through her hair.

I've been waiting for weeks to get a call like this. Why don't I feel happier?

CHAPTER 27

"Alright, everyone, let's get this house decked out in Christmas cheer." Evelyn paced back and forth in front of a large crew of workers who stood outside Frost Manor. The driveway was filled with cars and work trucks as her team descended upon the house. "Christmas is right around the corner. We need to get this place done as quickly and efficiently as possible. Let's make this house the community gem it used to be. Pierre, let's bring out more lights." Evelyn's heels clicked on the asphalt as she made notes on her clipboard and delegated jobs to the team.

Belle watched from the porch. The book *A Christmas Carol* was clutched in her cold fingers. Once everyone got to work, her next task was to thoroughly examine the first edition again to see what clue Sam could have hidden among the antique pages. Heading inside, Belle went to check on Ivy who was working with the interior design team. The inside of Frost Manor had been transformed into a bustling workplace; boxes and ladders were everywhere.

"Belle." Ivy appeared in the foyer and waved her over. "I want to get your opinion on the ideas I have for the ballroom." Ivy was dressed similar to her sister, only her blazer and pants were emerald. The same Christmas tree pin was attached to her lapel. Ivy went over her plan as they walked to the magnificent space. "I was thinking of putting two large poinsettia trees on either side of the entrance."

"I like that idea," replied Belle.

"We can place twelve trees around the room to represent the twelve days of Christmas. We can hang crystal snowflakes from the ceiling and weave garland in the chandeliers." Ivy pointed to each area as she explained her plan.

"That sounds lovely," replied Belle. "We can get the trees from the Frost Farm. I'm sure Jake won't have a problem with that."

"That's a wonderful idea! We'll transform this place into a Christmas spectacular," Ivy assured her.

As Belle exited the ballroom and headed to the solarium, the workers bustled around her carrying ladders and boxes into the different rooms. One of the employees came a little too close to Belle and bumped her arm. The collision caused her to stumble sideways, and she let go of the book. It clattered to the ground and her heart dropped.

"Sorry," the worker called over his shoulder.

Belle winced as she saw the almost two-hundred-year-old book lying on the ground. She hoped it hadn't been damaged. As she bent down to pick it up, she noticed a slight bulge in the spine.

Panic filled her as she rushed through the hall to the solarium. She closed the door and the smell of roses surrounded her. Belle stared at the cloth spine and tapped her finger against it. The hard bump moved. *That's weird.* She pressed her fingers against the bump and felt it move away from the pressure again. "This isn't part of the book." Putting both of her thumbs against the ridge, Belle continued to move her fingers in an upward motion, pushing the hidden object to the top. As she reached the edge of the spine, a piece of metal emerged from the opening.

It was a key.

"This must be the next clue." Turning the key over in her hand, she saw the letters A.F. engraved near the top of the key.

Agnes Frost?

Belle sprinted out the back door and across the yard to the first barn. "Jake!"

Jake stepped out of the nearby stall as she entered. He leaned the pitchfork against the wall. "What's wrong?"

Belle held the key up to show him. "I found the next clue! This was hidden in the spine of the book. It has the initials A.F. on it. Your grandmother's initials."

Jake took the key from her fingers and turned it over in his palm. He glanced up at the ceiling. Belle could see his mind working at a rapid pace, trying to remember what the key could be for.

"Did she have a jewelry box? Or a cabinet?" Belle looked around the barn. "Maybe something in here could be unlocked by it?"

"Was there a note?" he asked.

She shook her head. "Just the key."

"I'll have to think about it." Jake looked at the house. "Is the decorating company still here?"

"They'll be here all day. I figured you were out here since you don't like crowds."

"What gave you that idea?" Jake raised an eyebrow.

"You did. Hiding yourself away, rarely going into town, and getting all your necessities delivered." Belle chuckled.

"The internet is a beautiful thing, Belle. It's amazing what you can order directly to your door without ever having to leave the house." Jake took the wheelbarrow full of shavings and moved it aside. "But I suppose sometimes it's worth it to leave the house if it's with the right person." He turned to look at her. "Would you like to go get food while we wait for them to finish?"

"They're decorating the kitchen, Jake."

"I meant getting something in town to eat." Jake gave her a grin.

Belle felt her stomach grumble. She had skipped breakfast this morning in her rush to get to the manor. "I thought you didn't like leaving the house?"

"I don't, but for you, I'll make an exception."

A surge of excitement coursed through Belle, and a warm blush crept across her cheeks. "Yes, I would love to. There's a really cute coffee shop downtown. I can bring my laptop, and I can show you what we're doing for the Christmas Gala."

"I would love to see what you have planned for the gala." Jake placed the pitchfork back in the closet and wiped his hands on his jeans. "Let me get cleaned up and then we can go. Meet me by the garage in five minutes."

Belle couldn't stop smiling as she walked around the side of the house to the garage. She sat on the edge of the water fountain that was now filled with clear water, and admired the incredible progress being made on the exterior of the house. Half of the windows were covered in wreaths and festive garland, and the workers were outlining every part of the manor in lights.

"Ready to go?" Jake walked out the side door. He was black peacoat with a scarf wrapped around his neck. Belle paused for a minute admiring how handsome he was. "Do you want to take my car?" she gestured toward her vehicle.

"No, we'll take mine." Jake walked over to the garage that was attached to the mansion. He typed a code into the keypad, and within seconds, the heavy door retracted to reveal a white Range Rover SUV. The metallic paint shimmered in the sunlight. Jake pressed a button on the key fob, and the doors unlocked. He opened the passenger door and gestured for Belle to get inside. She slid into the ebony leather seats and noted how the interior of the vehicle was spotless. She could only dream of owning something so beautiful and elegant.

Jake closed her door for her and walked around the vehicle to get into the driver's seat. Starting the engine and backing out, they left the driveway and drove toward downtown.

CHAPTER 28

The aroma of freshly brewed coffee filled the air, and mingled with the enticing scent of baked goods. Soft jazz music played in the background. Sunlight streamed through the large windows, casting a glow on the polished wooden tables. Belle sat across from Jake in a booth at the Maple Walnut Café, in downtown Falls Village. Cups of coffee surrounded them along with scones and muffins. Her fingers tapped on the keyboard of her laptop while Jake looked over at the display case filled with an assortment of tempting pastries. Around them, people chatted over a hot drink, while others were engrossed in books or working at their computers.

"What do you think?" Belle turned her laptop toward Jake.

He leaned forward and stared at the screen. "The invitation looks stunning. *A Frost Family Charity Gala.* That has a nice ring to it. My grandparents always believed in giving back to others. Do we have enough time to get the word out though? The event is a week away."

Belle turned the screen back toward herself. "Falls Village sends out a weekly newsletter that discusses the events happening in the town. My parents are good friends with the mayor. I will have city hall send the invitation out with the newsletter this afternoon. I'll also post the notice on the town's social media pages. I have family and friends who will post it on their socials, too, and I'm going to email a copy to our local newspaper to run it in tomorrow's issue. We'll blast it all week long." Belle pulled a notebook out of her purse. "We have the decorations and food taken care of. My mother knows a string quartet willing to play at the event. One of my friends is going to provide us with table rentals as well as the chair coverings, and my godmother already had a handful of people sign up to donate items to the silent auction."

"Silent auction?" Jake raised an eyebrow.

"Yes. In addition to the ticket sales, the proceeds from the silent auction will go to charity." Belle closed the lid of her laptop.

"Wow, Belle, you've nailed it! It's exactly how my grandparents described the gala."

"I don't understand why your grandparents never held the gala at their home before." Belle took a sip of her coffee.

"I don't know. I guess they felt the manor, the Wishing Bell, and the tree lot got so much attention they wanted another location to get recognition." Jake shrugged. He handed his credit card to the waitress to pay before turning back to Belle. "Did you want to take a walk through downtown? I haven't had a chance to see much of Falls Village since I moved here."

"I would like that." Butterflies fluttered in Belle's stomach as Jake helped her put on her coat.

Remember: Jake's sworn off love. You're going to get your heart broken. Her thoughts plagued her. Yet, Belle couldn't control the palpitations in her chest whenever he showed her his sweet side.

Jake accepted his card back from the waitress and then offered Belle his arm. "Shall we?"

"Of course." Belle linked her arm with his.

As they stepped outside, Belle could feel the eyes of the passersby as they watched her walking with the Beast of Frost Manor. Many of them she had grown up with. While they gave her a smile and wave as they passed, Belle knew she would be the topic at their dinner tables tonight. But she didn't care. For the first time in a long time, she felt at peace and happy.

Downtown Falls Village was a picturesque scene, decked out in elaborate Christmas cheer. The buildings' vibrant colors contrasted against the crisp winter air. The lamp posts were decorated with garland and wreaths. Lights that resembled snowflakes hung in an arch above the street. Children's eyes sparkled with excitement as they gazed at the enchanting holiday displays in the store windows.

"This reminds me of the Christmas displays at Rockefeller Center," Jake said, glancing around at the decorations.

The aroma of roasted chestnuts and sweet treats filled the air, mingling with the sounds of laughter and joyful chatter. In the center square, the annual Falls Village Christmas Tree stood proudly decorated with beautiful glass ornaments and twinkling lights.

"It's stunning, isn't it?" said Belle as they stood in front of the towering tree.

"Yes, it is," Jake replied as they continued to walk down the holiday-covered streets. "Are you bringing a date to the gala?"

His random question took her by surprise. "No, I'm not."

"Really. I figured a woman of your stature would have a significant other."

"You say this as we're walking down the street together arm-in-arm." Belle laughed. "Besides, I don't think anyone is going to want a woman who is unemployed."

"Don't talk about yourself like that. You're a beautiful, talented woman, Belle. You're going to get another job," Jake assured her.

"I have a virtual interview tomorrow for a gallery in the city." Out of the corner of her eye, Belle thought she saw a look of disappointment flash across Jake's face. Belle looked down at her boots clicking against the brick sidewalk. "My last relationship was about a year ago. We were so busy with our careers that we barely saw each other, and we drifted apart. After that, I became so engrossed in running the gallery and working toward a promotion that there was never any time to date." She took a deep breath. "How about you, Jake? When was your last relationship?"

Jake looked over at one of the store windows as they walked past. "Two years ago. We were engaged. Let's just say it didn't end well."

"I'm sorry."

"Yeah. Me too." Jake's eyes glistened with emotion. "That's the wish I made."

"What?" Belle looked at him.

"When I first met my ex-fiancé, I was sure she was the one. I made a wish on the Wishing Bell that she would be my wife. As you can see, it didn't come true."

"You can't blame the Wishing Bell, Jake," Belle replied.

"Isn't the bell known for making your wishes come true? If the bell is truly magical, what I ask for should come true." He shook his head. "Life is crazy. You can spend years thinking you know someone, and the whole time she is wearing a mask. Then out of the blue, things change and she doesn't love you anymore. All the love I poured into our relationship was for nothing and I ended up with a broken heart."

"I don't know if I would look at love like that. Maybe the wish didn't come true because you were meant for someone better," replied Belle.

Jake snorted. "Everyone always says that when you get your heart broken."

"Love is a beautiful thing when both people are on the same page," continued Belle.

"And when they're not, the pain becomes too much to bear. That's why I won't ever fall in love again and why I believe the Wishing Bell is a bunch of nonsense."

"Jake, don't think like that," Belle scolded him.

They walked back to the square and stopped in front of the massive Christmas tree. Silence fell over them. Belle glanced at Jake who seemed lost in his own world. A light flurry of snowflakes came down in a passing shower. The white crystals decorated their coats and hair.

Jake snapped to attention. "I can't believe I forgot!" He unraveled his arm from Belle's and reached into his coat pocket to pull out the monogrammed key. "This key did belong to my grandmother. It unlocks her cabin."

"What cabin?" Belle turned to face him.

"When my grandparents got married, they inherited Frost Manor. My grandfather built my grandmother a beautiful log cabin on our property in the woods. My grandmother loved nature, and she was a sculptor. All those beautiful statues that are around the manor are her creations."

"That's impressive; she was a very talented woman." Belle remembered the grand hall of the manor filled with statues of various animals.

"My grandfather built her that cabin as an art studio for her to work in," Jake continued, placing the key back into his pocket. "Despite the ample room in the manor, Grandma wanted a separate place outside in nature where she could have peace and quiet. When my father was little he loved camping, so the cabin served as a place for the family to explore. I remember going there a few times when I was a child. I haven't been to the cabin at all since I moved into the house. I forgot it was even there."

"Where is it located?" Belle asked. "Is there a path to take?"

"The only way to get there is by horse. There are no roads for the cars, and I've never taken the snowmobiles that far. Grandpa was always adamant that sleigh rides were the best way because it allowed the soul to be one with nature." Jake snapped his fingers. "We can use the sleigh in the barn. Do you want to go now?"

"Absolutely. I need to know if this scavenger hunt is finally going to end or if we are getting another clue. Besides, it's a great way to pass the time since the crew will still be decorating when we return." Belle cried. She was filled with anticipation.

As they walked back to the SUV, Belle's excitement turned to disappointment. It was clear Jake's heart remained firmly closed on the subject of love.

CHAPTER 29

When they returned to the manor, Jake hurried to hitch up the sleigh. Belle went for a stroll around the mansion to check on the decorations. Slowly but surely the manor was transforming into a winter wonderland. She was excited to see the final product. Her boots crunched in the snow as she headed toward the barn. The wind whipped her scarf behind her and the chilling air froze her cheeks. But nothing took her breath away like what she saw waiting for her. In front of the barns stood Sam Frost's sleigh harnessed to two Clydesdale horses.

"Hello there friends," Belle cooed as she approached the horses.

The majestic draft horses towered over her. Their muscles rippled under their brown coats. Raising their elegant heads high, they sniffed the air, and stomped their giant hooves. She ran her gloved hand down the white strip on their faces and stroked their soft noses. As Belle moved closer to the sleigh, she saw that its dusty exterior was now bright and shiny. The red paint was glossy and the silver runners were freshly waxed. The seats had been vacuumed and a quilt was folded neatly on top.

"What do you think?" Jake appeared behind her.

"Jake. This is stunning. You know how to harness horses?" Belle gasped.

Jake smiled. "Don't doubt my abilities. My grandpa did teach me a thing or two."

"How did you clean up the sleigh so quickly?"

"I've had trouble sleeping the past few weeks, so I spent my nights refurbishing it. Jingle kept me company." Jake replied as he patted one of the Clydesdales' necks. "This is Bud and his brother Peppermint. They were Grandpa's favorites." Jake walked over to the side of the sleigh. "Ready to head to the cabins?" He held out his hand.

Belle placed her fingers in his. "Absolutely." She stepped into the sleigh and settled onto the seat. Jake climbed up beside her and spread a green quilt over their laps. He placed his fingers to his lips and let out a whistle. Jingle dashed across the backyard. The Saint Bernard paused by the sleigh, letting out a loud bark.

"Come on, Jingle." Jake gestured to the space behind them.

Taking a huge leap, Jingle jumped into the sleigh next to Jake, then hopped into the back. Jake clicked his tongue and moved the reins. Bud and Peppermint walked forward and with a lurch the sleigh was in motion. They crossed the yard and entered the woods.

Belle looked around at the bare trees dressed in icicles and the evergreen shrubs coated with snow as they passed the Christmas tree lots. "I'm impressed that you know how to drive a sleigh."

"There's a lot you don't know about me." Jake grinned.

"I've told you a lot about myself, but you haven't shared much about yourself," Belle hinted.

"You're right. I haven't." Jake stared ahead at the snowy countryside and took a deep breath. "When I lived in New York City, I fell in love. I was an entrepreneur starting up my software company, and she was an intern on Wall Street. Over time, she became a senior associate in wealth management. We were together for seven years. Two years ago, we were supposed to get married on Christmas Eve at Saint Patrick's Cathedral, with a reception at The Plaza." He paused. "When the day arrived, I stood at the altar with my groomsmen and her bridesmaids. We waited and waited, but she never showed. It turns out she left me a note in her dressing room telling me that she couldn't go through with the wedding. She ran off to California to be with her ex-boyfriend that she had been cheating on me with for the last three years."

Mournful silence surrounded them and Belle felt miserable. The whole town of Falls Village had judged Jake for his frosty exterior, when in reality he was a man with a broken heart.

Jake's grip tightened on the reins. "I had a gut feeling she was cheating on me. I only wish I had listened to myself, but I guess I didn't want to believe she would do that to me. It would have been nice if she would have told me beforehand, instead of making me stand at the altar like an idiot for almost an hour. She broke my heart and embarrassed me in front of all my family and friends. After that horrible fiasco, I decided that relationships weren't for me. I would focus on myself. That's why I spray painted the rose in the solarium black. My ex-fiancé wanted roses lining the church aisle, rose arrangements on every table at the reception, and rose petals everywhere. Roses may have been my grandfather's passion, but for me they are nothing but heartbreak; a phantom limb of love that refuses to fade."

"I'm so sorry, Jake," Belle whispered. She reached over and patted Jake's arm. She wished she knew the right words to take away his pain. Now she understood his beastly manner. Heartbreak was a tempestuous storm that raged within his soul.

Jake pulled back on the reins and slowed the horses to a stop. "Here we are." He gestured toward a luxurious log cabin surrounded by pine trees. Draped in a blanket of snow, the cabin stood proudly against the wintry backdrop. The sea of towering pines surrounded the rustic structure. A sprawling two-tiered porch wrapped around the front of the cabin.

As Belle stepped down from the sleigh, her eyes caught sight of a family of deer grazing near a cluster of evergreens. Their elegant heads rose to look at them. "This place is beautiful," she exclaimed.

"I always thought so too." Jake tied the reins to a nearby tree.

With a loud woof, Jingle jumped out of the sleigh. His abrupt action startled the deer and they scampered deeper into the forest. The massive dog sniffed around the front of the cabin.

"Jingle, stay here and keep the horses company." Jake took the key out of his pocket. "Let's see what Grandpa wanted us to find."

Together, they stepped onto the quaint front porch. Next to the front door was a weathered porch swing dusted in snow. Jake fit the key into the lock and the door swung open. Belle stepped onto the shiny wood floors and looked around.

The interior of the cabin was a harmonious blend of rustic charm and contemporary comfort. Exposed, hand-hewn beams criss-crossed the high cathedral ceilings. The walls were painted the color of golden honey. In the living room was a stone fireplace flanked by built-in bookshelves. Soft, oversize leather sofas were covered with dust sheets and the large windows offered a panoramic view of the surrounding forest. In front of the bay window was a large Christmas tree decorated for the upcoming holiday. Strings of unlit lights peeked through the needles and various ornaments had been placed on the limbs. Belle reached out and touched the soft branches with her fingers. There wasn't a fragrance of pine, and when she tried to bend one of the needles it wouldn't break. This tree was faux.

"Why is there a fake tree in this room?" she asked.

"I don't know. I haven't been here in a very long time," replied Jake as he walked into the kitchen.

Belle looked around at the rustic iron chandeliers, handwoven rugs, and pieces of nature-inspired art. Statues and pottery created by Jake's grandmother were scattered throughout the place. She took a step forward, and felt something brush against her boot. Looking down, she saw two boxes hidden beneath the tree. One was a large square box wrapped in glossy emerald paper. The other was a small rectangular box covered in vibrant crimson wrapping. Both presents were adorned with matching gold ribbons. On top of the red gift were two letters, and on top of the green box was a wooden sign. Belle took the two boxes and placed them on the coffee table.

"Jake, come here."

Jake's boots clunked against the wood floor as he entered the living room. "What is it?"

"This must be what Sam wanted us to find." Belle handed him an envelope. "There are two letters. One is addressed to me and the other is addressed to you."

"Me?" Jake took the letter and looked at the print. He stuffed it into the inside pocket of his coat. "I can read it later. He picked up the wooden sign and read the fancy calligraphy, "'Home is not a place. Home is a person.' Hmmm that's an interesting take. I wonder what's in these boxes? Let's open them."

"Don't you want to know what the letters say? Maybe we'll finally get some answers about why he led us on this scavenger hunt?" Belle asked.

Jake grimaced. "I would rather open the gifts first." He picked up the bigger box.

"Alright." Belle reluctantly folded her envelope and put it in her coat pocket. She was dying to know what Sam had written. However, she felt funny reading the letter if Jake wasn't going to read his. She had a feeling they were meant to be read together. She picked up the red box.

Jake dug his fingers into the emerald paper and tore off the wrapping. He opened the lid to reveal the missing clapper. "Now we know where the missing clapper went."

Belle felt a wave of relief wash over her as she stared at the long rod with the circular ball at the end. She brushed her fingers along the cold exterior of the clapper. "I don't understand. Why would Sam send us on a wild goose chase only to have the clapper wrapped up like a gift?"

"There was always a method to Grandpa's madness," replied Jake. He nodded at the gift in Belle's hands.

Belle ripped away the tightly wrapped paper and opened the gift to find a smaller one inside. Removing the cover revealed a gold chain with a pendant that was heart-shaped with diamonds along the edge. Peering closer, Belle saw engraved inside the heart was a small bell. She took the chain out of the box and held it up to the light.

"That was my grandmother's necklace." Jake cupped his hand around the heart pendant and looked closer. "I haven't seen this in years. Sam must've wanted you to have it."

"Me?" Belle shook her head. "Are you sure it's not for you? After all, you are his grandson."

"What am I going to do with it? Grandpa gave that chain to my grandma who was a beautiful woman, and it should be another beautiful woman who wears it now."

A blush crept over Belle's face. "I can't accept this. This is a priceless heirloom that belongs to your family. This necklace must be close to eighty years old."

"I'm sure Grandpa would want you to have it," Jake insisted.

Belle reached into her pocket and took out the envelope. "I don't understand the significance of these two items. The answer must be in the letters. We have to open them." Just as she was about to slide her thumb under the lip to break the seal, the phone rang.

Evelyn's name came up on the screen.

Disappointed in the timing, Belle placed the call on speaker. "Hi Evelyn."

"Hi Belle. Is Jake with you?"

"Yes, he is. Would you like to speak with him?" Belle looked at Jake who was vigorously shaking his head.

"No, that's alright. I wanted to call to let you know that we have finished decorating the house. Both the interior and the exterior are complete. And I must say, we did an excellent job. The place looks stunning!" gushed Evelyn.

"That's wonderful! We'll head back to Frost Manor and I'll give you the check," Belle replied.

"No need for that. Jake already paid us. I wanted to know when you'll be here to take a look," Evelyn explained.

"We'll be there in about fifteen minutes," replied Belle.

"Excellent. Let me know your thoughts once you have taken everything in. If you want any changes, we can come back tomorrow to make them."

"Thank you, Evelyn." Belle hung up the phone.

"The manor is finished?" Jake raised his eyebrow.

"Yes." Belle placed her phone in her pocket. "You paid the decorators?"

"Of course."

"But I told you I would take care of everything. That was part of our deal," Belle explained.

"Nonsense. What kind of a man would I be if I had a woman paying for my decorations?" Jake placed his hands on Belle's shoulders and turned her to the door. "Now, let's head back so we can see the miraculous transformation of the manor. And maybe, if I'm lucky, Falls Village will finally stop giving me grief about it not being decorated."

CHAPTER 30

A gasp escaped Belle's lips as the sleigh rounded the corner and Frost Manor came into view. The crown jewel of Christmas was back.

Tiny lights shaped like stars lined the driveway. Every tree and bush on the property had been covered in festive lights. The base of the water fountain was filled with red water beads, and each of the basins above it were layered with sprigs of holly, evergreen, and gingham bows. The reindeer statue at the top had a collar of berries around its neck, and stars on its antlers. A life-size reindeer pulling a sleigh had been placed on the left side of the yard, and Santa statue sat inside with its hand poised in a wave. There was a nativity scene, complete with baby Jesus, Mary, Joseph, shepherds, and the three wise men, as well as an assembly of donkeys, oxen, cows, sheep, and camels. Giant nutcrackers had been placed in between the juniper trees and tall snowmen lined the property.

Evelyn and her team had departed, leaving them to enjoy the beauty of the mansion alone. Jake stopped the sleigh in front of the barn and helped Belle down. Together, they unharnessed the horses, groomed them, and placed them in their stalls. Then Jake pushed the sleigh into the equipment barn. Arm-in-arm, they walked toward the mansion. The peaks and roof of Frost Manor were outlined in lights. The pillars were wrapped in garland. Wreaths hung from every window and candles were positioned inside the panes. Poinsettia plants lined the edges of the stairs that led to the front door. Belle's eyes welled with tears and she brushed them away with her hand. A few weeks ago, a part of her had felt like the nostalgic ambiance of the manor had been lost forever, but instead, it had been reincarnated.

"It's almost like Grandpa decorated the place himself," Jake murmured, as he gazed up at the windows. He walked up the steps to the house and opened the door. Belle stepped into the foyer, and her jaw dropped at the elaborate holiday display that stood before her. Garland had been strung down the double staircases, and fully decorated trees stood next to the banisters with wrapped boxes beneath it.

The dining room had garland, berries, and candy canes hanging from the chandelier, and an elaborate centerpiece made of pine boughs, pine cones, and candles sat on the table. Each room they strolled through, from the kitchen to the bathroom to the bedroom, had its own Christmas tree. The pines ranged from short to tall. Wreaths, garlands, candy canes, poinsettias, snowflakes, and icicles had turned the ghostly mansion into a winter wonderland.

The last place they visited was the ballroom. Pine trees made of poinsettias had been placed on either side of the double doors, along with two wreaths hanging from the trim. Belle opened the doors and stared in awe at the beauty of the room that would host the Christmas Gala. Garland, snowflakes, and lights had been strung across the ceiling, and the double chandelier had candy canes hanging from its curves. The wooden dance floor was glossy and ready to host crowds of dancers. Around the outside of the dance floor, multiple circular tables had been set up with red coverings. A gold runner ran along the center of each table. On top of each runner was a tall centerpiece vase that held a bouquet of poinsettias and evergreens. Crystals hung from the arrangements and candles surrounded the vases. Each chair had a ruby covering with a gold sash tied into a bow. On the left side of the ballroom, tables had been set up for the buffet, and on the right side were the displays for the silent auction. Surrounding the room were twelve Christmas trees that were decorated with different themes ranging from candy canes to gingerbread. On the far wall, a backdrop panel filled with greenery and red roses had been placed to use as a photo op, and off to the side was a fully stocked bar.

"I'm really impressed," Jake said, breaking the silence. "I never imagined this place could ever look this good without my grandfather's touch. He would be so happy to see it this way."

"Sam would be so proud that you decided to decorate, and I'm proud of you too," Belle said as they walked out of the ballroom and down the corridor toward the living room, kitchen, and dining area.

"Surprisingly, I'm actually looking forward to the ball. I even invited a few friends from the city to come," Jake revealed.

"Jake, that's wonderful. I'm happy to hear that." The ding of a notification made Belle stop in the doorframe to the living room. She pulled out her phone. "Our announcement about the Christmas Gala is gaining a lot of traction on social media. Over five hundred people have reshared the post. Josie sent me a message saying the gala is the talk of the town. Everyone wants to come and celebrate the Frost legacy."

"Belle," Jake said.

"Yes?" Belle slid her phone back in her pocket and stared up at Jake. A content expression crossed his face, but he remained silent. "What's wrong?" Belle watched his eyes flicker between her lips and the top of the doorframe. Following his gaze, Belle felt her heart beat so loud she was sure Jake could hear it. Hanging down above them was a ball of mistletoe on a green string. Belle quickly looked down at her boots, unsure of how to address the timeless tradition.

Everything stood still as Jake took a step toward her, closing the distance between them until his body was inches from hers. He reached up and cupped his hands around her lower jaw, tilting her face to him. His green eyes held her captive as a cosmic pull drew them closer. A drumbeat echoed in Belle's veins as their faces were inches apart. Their breaths mingled in the hushed air until finally their lips touched. Belle closed her eyes, giving in to every suppressed feeling she had for him. Kissing Jake was the equivalent of sipping hot chocolate with marshmallows and whipped cream after hours in the cold. The sweetness on her tongue and lips chased out the chill that had been buried in her bones. It was as if she had been missing something for a very long time and had finally found it. The kiss lasted for a while until Jake pulled back abruptly. He drew Belle close to him so her head was against his chest. She could feel his muscles tense.

Stepping out of the embrace he murmured, "I'm sorry Belle." Then he vanished like the petal of a rose carried off by the winter wind. Belle was left shivering in his absence, the warmth of his touch a distant memory, as her heart fell to the floor and cracked open.

CHAPTER 31

A stroke of crimson across the blank canvas triggered Belle's memory of her passionate kiss with Jake. She had spent most of the afternoon and well into the evening in the barn loft, painting to her heart's content. Her mind replayed their interaction over and over. After he abruptly ended their kiss, Jake had retired to the secret corners of Frost Manor. Belle thought it best to leave early and let him be alone with his emotions. Even though his reaction had tainted the moment, Belle couldn't deny how the warmth of his lips against hers made her feel more alive than ever before.

"How are you doing, honey?" Her dad's heavy work boots echoed against the wood floors of the loft. He paused. "You're going for the abstract approach. I like it."

"I'm trying to portray the complexity of love," replied Belle half-jokingly.

Her father pulled up a chair and sat down beside her. "Does this have something to do with Jake?" His eyebrows raised.

"Maybe." A small giggle slipped from Belle's lips.

A knowing smile crossed her dad's face. "Love is a complex emotion. It can be beautiful and it can be painful. It can make you feel alive and other times it can make you feel dead." He turned to her. "What seems to be the issue?"

"Well, I like Jake and I believe he likes me too, but he experienced some heartbreak in the past and I think it's preventing him from being open to love."

"Are you sure about that?" asked her dad.

"He keeps a black rose in his solarium to remind him of his choice to never fall in love again," Belle recited.

Her father cringed. "His past breakup was that bad?"

Belle nodded.

"Heartbreak is one of the only injuries that manifests in the physical, but is purely emotional. Even though your mind says your heart is broken and you feel like your heart is broken, the heart continues to beat at the same pace and rhythm with no changes."

"Jake blames the Wishing Bell for not granting his wish to be with the person who broke his heart," confessed Belle.

"Wishes can be complicated when they involve another person. You can't control others. You can only control yourself. Oftentimes a wish doesn't come true because the universe feels you deserve better."

"You're right. I only wish Jake could see that," replied Belle.

Her father's comforting hand found her shoulder as he stood up. "He'll figure it out." Then he walked out of the loft, leaving her alone with her paintings and her thoughts.

Belle drummed her fingers on the closed laptop as she sat at the desk in the office of her parents' farmhouse. It was the next morning, and her video interview with the Chenello Museum had just finished. Overall, Belle felt the meeting had gone well. The board seemed very impressed with her resume and experience. However, Belle didn't feel fulfilled. A few months ago, the idea of working at a prestigious gallery would have excited her, but now she dreaded the thought of leaving Vermont.

Maybe the small town lifestyle was growing on her or maybe she had moved past the feelings of rejection about her art that had caused her to leave in the first place. Deep in her heart, she knew her interactions with Jake had a lot to do with her change of feelings. Her rampant thoughts had fueled her decision to skip going to the manor today. The number one reason was she wasn't sure how to address the kiss yesterday or her feelings for Jake. A part of her hoped he felt the same way, but she was scared of rejection. A whirlwind of emotions swept through Belle as she grabbed her keys and headed to the bakery.

Thirty minutes later, Belle stood at one of the ovens in the kitchen at Plum Kiss Desserts. Her hand clenched the handle as she waited for the last few seconds to time out before she could open the door. Around her, the other employees chatted about what they were going to wear and who they were going to take to the gala. Belle was pleased. The Christmas Gala was bringing much needed attention to their little town. The last time Belle went over the details with Josie, there were over five hundred people who had RSVP'd to attend the event. They had come to the conclusion that they would need to add more desserts to their menu. Maybe even a hot chocolate bar. Her coworkers' laughs filled the air as they boxed orders and restocked the display cases. Belle wished she could share in their joy. The timer brought her back to reality. She opened the oven, removed multiple trays of gingerbread cookies, and placed them on the cooling racks.

"Belle!" Josie entered the kitchen and grabbed Belle's arm.

"What's wrong, Josie?" Belle placed her mittens on the shelf.

"Pasquale Fontana is here. I can't believe it," Josie squealed.

"Who?"

"Pasquale Fontana--he was one of Sam's best friends, remember? I told you this the other day." Josie squeezed Belle's arm tighter.

"That's right. I remember now."

"He's here." Josie dragged her toward the doors. "He's sitting in one of the booths near the window. He just ordered a coffee and a piece of cheesecake. This is a sign. He hasn't come to town in months, and now, here he is."

"What do you want me to do?" Belle peeked through one of the small windows and scanned the eating area.

"Take off your apron, go serve him his cheesecake, and ask him about Jake," replied Josie.

"I can't ask him about Jake," protested Belle.

"Why not?" Josie glared at her.

"Because that would be weird. He doesn't know who I am. You want me to walk up to him and ask him about his old friend's grandson? Besides, I already found out what I needed to know and it wasn't good."

"Oh please, stop being so dramatic." Josie untied the string of Belle's apron. "Then ask him about the scavenger hunt Sam sent you on. Just do it." With a strong shove, Josie pushed Belle through the doors into the cash register area.

"Alright." Belle groaned as Josie gave her a wink and disappeared back into the kitchen.

A few minutes later, Belle approached the booth by the window. She balanced a slice of cheesecake in one hand while trying not to spill the cup of coffee in the other.

Pasquale Fontana sat in a booth reading the newspaper. A burgundy flannel shirt and jeans clothed his plump body. His face was framed by a thick snow-white beard that almost touched his chest. His cheeks were round and rosy and there was a distinct twinkle in his blue eyes.

"Mr. Fontana?" Belle asked. She paused in disbelief. This man was a striking image of Santa Claus. It was like he had jumped out of a page from one of her childhood storybooks.

Pasquale took off the spectacles that were perched on his nose and laid them on the table. A smile spread across his face as he stood up and nodded. "Belle Winters. It's a pleasure to meet you." He extended his hand.

Belle placed the coffee and cheesecake on the table then shook his hand. She wasn't sure how he already knew her name. The old man gestured for her to take a seat across from him.

"You're the young lady we have to thank for transforming the manor back to its former glory. It's been a long time since I've seen the Christmas spirit in that place. And, most importantly, you tamed the Beast in Jake."

A rush of crimson spread across Belle's face as she slid into the booth. "What? How do you know that?"

Pasquale's hearty laugh echoed throughout the bakery and his smile wrinkled his eyes into crescents. "It's a small town, dear, and when it comes to Frost Manor, there's not much that I don't know about that place. Call me Pasquale. I have a feeling you want to ask me something."

Belle stared at Pasquale's beard that was full and soft like a cloud. She twisted a napkin between her hands. "It's about Sam and Jake."

"Of course it is. I've known them both for a long time. Sam was a jolly old soul. Bless his heart. Jake has always been a kind and caring man. It's a shame he still lives in the past."

"He told me about his fiancé leaving him at the altar two years ago at Christmas. Because of what happened, he doesn't believe in love, Christmas, or the Wishing Bell."

Pasquale folded his hands and looked at her. "Yes, Sam filled me in on the details of that horrible time in Jake's life. It's a shame how we as humans can be filled with so much joy and happiness, yet we allow one person who isn't even worth our time to take that away from us." He paused. "Do you wish to know if Jake's heart is broken beyond repair?"

"Something like that." Belle struggled to explain.

"A heart can only be broken if the person allows it, just like a heart can be healed if a person believes." A smile spread across Pasquale's face. "You love Jake, don't you? And you want to know if he is capable of loving you back?"

"What?" Belle wished the ground would open and swallow her whole. "I mean...I like him...I care about him..."

"Hush, dear." Pasquale waved his hand. "Don't stress yourself out. You don't have to explain anything to me." He gave her a wink. "Jake is capable of loving again, once he stops being a prisoner to his past. You see, Belle, people who seem to have a beastly attitude and are unkind, were once people who cared too much. Many times, when a broken heart has been silenced, it takes a special person to get it to beat again. Concerning Jake, I know that special person is you."

"Me?" Belle thought about the kiss they shared then how Jake had run off like a departing north wind.

"When Jake first met Madison, she was down on her luck. During their relationship, he did everything for her. He helped her not only get back on her feet but achieve so much more than she would have alone. When she was able to stand on her own, instead of remembering the person who had helped her when she had nothing, she believed she was too good for him and left in the cruelest way possible. Since that day, I've never seen Jake glance in another woman's direction until he saw you," explained Pasquale.

Belle tried to absorb the moment of flattery, but curiosity struck her. "Wait, when did you see us?"

Pasquale chuckled, his blue eyes twinkling. "There's something else gnawing at you. What is it?"

"When Sam passed away, he left me an ornament that looks like the Wishing Bell. When I examined the real bell, I discovered it was missing its clapper, and there was a note. It turns out Sam hid clues throughout Frost Manor to lead us to the location of the clapper. At the end of the scavenger hunt we found a necklace and letters. I just don't understand the point of all of it."

"Jake helped you with the riddles?" asked Pasquale.

"Yes."

The jolly man smiled. "Maybe the point was to show you that you don't always have to do everything alone, Belle."

"What do you mean?"

Pasquale took a sip of his coffee. "Last time I checked, it's been a while since you opened your heart and let love find its way to your soul. I know all your past relationships ended amicably, but time has made you feel like you can only do things better by yourself. While that is a great attitude to have, it's always better to have a genuine person in your corner."

Belle drummed her fingers on the table. "Let me get this straight. Sam did all of this to tell me that I can't do everything alone? Did he tell you he was going to do this?"

Pasquale stood up and put on his red coat. "I know you're feeling lost right now, Belle. Sometimes, when obstacles are put in our way, it pushes us to be exactly where we need to be. Remember, we don't know what we're capable of until we try, and we will never know how a person truly feels about us until we ask." Giving her a nod, he strolled toward the door. With his hand on the handle, he paused. "Oh and one last thing, dear. Read the letter." Then he was gone.

Calmness washed over Belle and her eyes widened in enlightenment. A veil of clarity had chased away the confusion surrounding her heart. Pasquale was right. She needed to talk to Jake. She needed to take a leap of faith and tell him how she felt.

She stood up and walked over to the kitchen door. "Josie?"

Her sister opened the door immediately, making it apparent she had been eavesdropping. "What happened? Are you alright?"

"I don't know. Pasquale made a lot of good points in our conversation. I need to go talk to Jake." Belle grabbed her coat.

"Of course! Don't worry, we have everything covered here. Are you going to make up with Jake?" Hope glistened in Josie's eyes.

"We aren't even together, Josie." Belle rolled her eyes.

"But that might change after you talk." Josie leaned against the door.

A smile crept across Belle's face. "I hope so."

CHAPTER 32

Belle's heart skipped a beat every time Frost Manor came into view. To see the mansion decked out in Christmas cheer brought joy to her heart. Belle parked her car in front of the door. Jake was beneath the windows of the manor, trimming the blue holly bushes that framed the exterior. Putting the car in park, Belle watched Jake move in a rhythmic grace with the shears. His brow furrowed in concentration as he studied each limb, making precise cuts. Belle quickly got out of the car and walked toward him before she lost her nerve. If she was offered the job in the city, Jake's feelings toward her would be a determining factor in whether or not she accepted it.

"Jake," she called.

"Belle?" Jake backed out of the bushes, brushing dead leaves off his arm. "What are you doing here?" A smile crossed his face as he walked over to her. "I mean, I'm glad to see you, but I thought you texted me that you weren't coming here today."

"I needed to talk to you," Belle began. She looked down and saw strings of lights scattered across the ground. "What are you doing?"

"Last night I noticed the lights wrapped around these holly bushes weren't projecting enough light. Turns out the bushes needed a trim. Now I'm adjusting the lights so they'll shine brighter."

"I'll help you." Belle placed her phone on the front steps. Her nerves had won after all.

Jake handed her a string of lights. "You can cover that bush right there and I'll work on this one."

"Okay." Belle walked over to the third bush on the left.

They worked in silence. Belle tried to concentrate on winding the lights through the red berries, but the kiss with Jake yesterday was gnawing at her. Jake hadn't said anything about it and was acting like nothing had happened. She needed to tell him how she felt even if he didn't feel the same. But she was unsure where to begin. On the way over, Belle had repeated over and over in her head what she was going to say, but now she couldn't remember anything.

The crisp winter air nipped at Belle's exposed skin as she crouched down to grab the last string of lights. Her fingers ached, as she weaved the lights through the dense branches. When she tugged on a stubborn strand, her hand slipped and collided with the shiny serrated leaves. She gasped in pain. Withdrawing her hand from the bush, she saw a bead of blood appear on the side of her palm.

"What happened?" Jake was by her side.

"My hand caught the sharp side of the holly leaf. I forgot how pointy they can be. It's like a papercut." Belle reached into her jacket pocket and pulled out a tissue to dab the blood.

"I'll get you a band-aid and some hydrogen peroxide." Jake moved to head inside.

A loud ring sounded from Belle's phone on the steps. It was probably the woman from the interview. The company had said they would be calling her around this time. Belle pulled her keys from her pocket and handed them to Jake. "There are band-aids in the glovebox of my car. Please grab one for me. I have to answer this call."

Jake nodded and took her keys as Belle ran to the front steps and grabbed her phone.

Belle placed the device to her ear. "Hello?"

"Good afternoon. May I speak to Miss Winters?" a female's voice responded.

"This is her."

"Hello Miss Winters, this is Sofia Beaumont from the Chenello Museum of Art. I'm calling to let you know that after your interview earlier today, we decided that the position of Director of Marketing would not be a good fit for you."

Belle's heart sank. "Thank you for the opportunity." She felt Jake's presence next to her. He held out his hand for hers, and she eagerly placed her palm in his.

"I'm not finished yet. We believe that you're a better fit for a different position. Vice-President of the museum," continued Sofia.

"What?" Belle was flabbergasted. She heard Jake open the wrapper of the band-aid.

"We feel that your expertise, enthusiasm, and demeanor is exactly what we need in the Vice-President position," continued Sofia.

Belle winced as Jake rubbed her cut with a cloth soaked in hydrogen peroxide. "I'm honored. I appreciate it," she exclaimed.

"I know this is a big shock for you. I'll send over the paperwork to your email in about twenty minutes. We'll give you time to look over the proposal and decide if it's to your liking. If you have any questions, you can contact me," finished Sofia.

Jake placed the band-aid over Belle's cut.

"Thank you so much. I will look it over right away. Thank you. Have a great day. Goodbye." Belle ended the call. "Thank you, Jake. I wanted to say..." Belle turned to look at him and was startled by the angry look on his face.

"What's this?" Jake held up the cracked portrait of the blonde woman that had been wedged under his arm.

Seeing the picture of the lady, Belle felt like she had plunged into icy cold water. Embarrassment washed over her and a hot blush rose to her cheeks. She had forgotten she had left the picture in the glove compartment. "Jake..."

"Why do you have this?" he snapped, not letting her finish.

"I found it in the attic."

"I found it in the attic too. Then I put it in the garbage. How did this picture get from the trash to your glove compartment?" Jake clutched the frame tightly in his hand.

"I put it there." Belle looked down at her boots.

"You went through my garbage?" He looked at her in disbelief. "Why Belle?"

"It's not like that," Belle began. "I was throwing away the empty dog food bag and there it was. There were so many secrets, I..."

"There were so many secrets that you made it a point to look through my garbage to figure it out?" Jake interrupted. He threw the portrait onto the asphalt.

The way he worded it made her feel like an idiot. She shouldn't have gotten involved. "I-I just wanted to help, Jake. You were sad and hurt. I wanted to know why you had sworn off love, and the black rose..."

"Since you're so curious to know my business, that's a picture of Madison, my ex-fiancé."

Belle could hear the bitterness in his words. "Why did you keep her portrait in the attic?"

"I forgot that I put it on my desk a long time ago. When I moved in, I stored my extra furniture and boxes in the attic." Jake waved his hands. "Seriously, do you always think you can do whatever you want?"

"What are you talking about?" Belle's voice cracked.

Jake's chin trembled. "You come to *my* house demanding to know why *my* house isn't decorated for Christmas. Then you make a deal with me because your family members vandalized my property. Now, I have a whole house decorated for Christmas and an upcoming gala, and I don't even know if I want all this."

"You gave me permission," Belle cried. "And what do you mean that I think I can do whatever I want? I"ll admit I may have been a little pushy about Christmas, but you came around and even enjoyed decorating. It's not my fault you got hurt and now you can't even celebrate a holiday because of it."

Jake took a deep breath. "Don't even go there, Belle. You don't know what it's like."

"We've all been hurt, Jake." Belle took a step closer to him. "Do you think I haven't had my heart broken before? Do you think you're the only one who got burned by someone they cared about? It's not always about love. Do you think I wanted to lose my job in the city? I trusted the people I worked with and they laid me off. But you don't shut yourself away in a mansion and get a cold heart. You pick yourself up and you keep going." Belle reached out and placed her hand on Jake's arm.

"You don't understand," Jake growled as he looked at the manor. "I didn't even want these stupid decorations. I only did it to make you happy."

"I appreciate that, Jake. But don't let the past consume you. You can move on, and you can love again. You proved that yesterday when we kissed," continued Belle.

Jake wrenched free from her grasp. "I don't understand, Belle. I trusted you. In the beginning I know I was evasive, and I wouldn't tell you why I refused to decorate the manor or why I tried to avoid Christmas. But eventually I did open up and tell you. Why did you feel the need to remove items from my garbage? Obviously they're there for a reason. I'm trying to forget the past and here I find my ex-fiancé's photo in your glove box. Why are you always meddling in things that don't concern you? Why can't you ever leave well enough alone?"

Belle hung her head.

"Besides, how can anything happen between us anyway? You're moving back to the city for your new job. I heard you on the phone. I'm not going back to New York City. My life is here."

"There is such a thing as a long-distance relationship, Jake," Belle replied.

Jake shook his head. "I did the long-distance thing with Madison when she was traveling for work. That's how she ended up cheating on me for years. I can't go through that again. I can't let my heart get broken." He bent down and picked up the portrait. "Now, I'm going to throw this picture in the garbage, and it's going to stay there this time."

Belle clenched her fists. "Fine. Maybe that will get you to stop thinking about someone who didn't deserve you. You think Madison is moping around and feeling bad for what she did to you? No, she isn't. She has a new man and has moved on with her life. It's about time you did the same." Belle reached over and took her keys from Jake's hand. "I'm leaving. I've fulfilled my promise to you, so there's no need for me to keep coming back here."

She didn't give him a chance to respond and stormed to her car. Without a backward glance, she sped away from Frost Manor, desperate to put as much distance between them as possible.

CHAPTER 33

Several days had passed since her heated argument with Jake. Feeling miserable, Belle had thrown herself into her painting. The Chenello Museum had told her that she could take a few days to think about their offer of employment. Belle thought it would be an easy decision to take the job in New York City. But the country life, more time with family, and Jake had made this choice rather difficult. In her moment of confliction, she escaped to the one thing that had always brought her clarity. Her painting. Belle moved her brush along the canvas, the colors blending together. Each stroke added peace to the turmoil she was feeling.

"How'd I know you'd be here," a sweet voice called.

Belle turned to see her mother coming up the stairs carrying a mug of hot chocolate.

"I brought you something warm to drink. I know this place can be a bit drafty." She placed the bright red mug on the table next to Belle.

"Thanks, Mom." Belle put her paintbrush down and picked up the cup. Steam rose from the cocoa, and the heat was a comfort against her hands.

"That's a pretty painting." Her mother sat down next to her and stared at the colorful canvas.

"It was supposed to be a gift for a friend." Belle looked down at the marshmallows floating in the creamy beverage.

"A friend like Jake?" her mother hinted.

"Mom. You know Jake and I aren't on good terms right now. I know it's my fault. I should have respected his wishes and left the portrait in the garbage. I shouldn't have meddled. But he was so unhappy. I thought if I could figure out who the woman was, I could understand his feelings and help him be happy again." Belle sighed. "And maybe I was a little bit jealous when I saw the photo." She had told her family the whole story when she had returned home after her argument with Jake. She took a sip of the hot chocolate and placed the cup back on the table.

"Sweetie, don't be so hard on yourself. I'm sure Jake has had time to think about what happened, and he knows you had good intentions. Love makes us go to extreme lengths to help the ones we care about," her mother assured her.

"What do you mean?" asked Belle.

"Honey, this whole family knows there's more than friendship between you and Jake. I'm your mother. I can tell by the way your face lights up when you talk about him, and how excited you've been to go to Frost Manor every day." Her mother smiled.

"Yes, I care for Jake and I like him. Things were going well until everything got complicated." Belle shook her head. "Everything is a mess. I thought I had my life planned out. I thought getting this new job was going to make me happy, but now I don't know if I want to go back to the city."

Her mother gave her a hug. "Sweetie, life is a journey, and it's never going to be easy. But here is the good thing. You may start out on one path, but it doesn't have to be the one you stay on forever. You're allowed to change your mind if something no longer makes you happy. That's the beauty of life. We are constantly growing and changing as people. Sometimes, we leave a particular path and come back to it later. You're allowed to want more for yourself. You have grown into a beautiful woman, and I couldn't be prouder of you. I want nothing more than for you to be happy."

Belle felt tears gathering in her eyes. She hugged her mother tight.

"Everything is going to work out, honey. You're going to figure it all out." Her mother rose from her chair. "I hope you're still planning on going to the Christmas Gala."

"I don't know," Belle sighed, her voice filled with doubt. "It'll be awkward between Jake and me."

"No, it won't," her mother replied firmly. "You two need to talk like adults and work things out, instead of acting like children and avoiding each other. I'm going to be there, your father will be there, and so will your siblings; there's no need for awkwardness. You were part of the planning process so you should see the fruits of your labor. And I know there is a handsome, beastly man who wants you to come even if he won't admit it." Her mother gave her shoulder a squeeze before leaving Belle to her thoughts.

Belle stared at the painting. Her Christmas gift for Jake was almost done, but should she even give it to him? Her mind drifted to the clapper and the necklace that was somewhere in Frost Manor. She still couldn't figure out the point behind this wild goose chase.

Read the letter.

Pasquale's words ran through her mind. With everything that had been going on, she had completely forgotten about it. Belle lunged for her jacket that had been thrown across a nearby chair. She stuck her hand in the pocket and retrieved the letter. She tore open the top and took out the note. Seeing Sam's words scrawled across the paper was a comfort she didn't know she needed.

My Dearest Belle,

I hope you find yourself in good health. If you are

reading this, then I know you decided to embark on the challenge I created for you. You have reached the end of my mystery, and I'm sure you are filled with questions. Why did I do this? What was the point? I will answer them all now.

Ever since you were a little girl helping your grandma tend to my roses, you shined with a light unlike any other. Your smile, your enthusiasm, your joy for life, it was evident you were destined for a great stage. Also, your artistic ability was unique and rare. The images you painted were stunning and brought happiness to others.

That is why it saddened me when you gave up your gift and lowered yourself for a job that didn't appreciate you. For years, when you came home for one day on the holidays, it broke my heart seeing you tired and over-worked. It angered me that you couldn't see you were meant for more than a corporate job.

A bell without its clapper is silenced. For many years, Belle, you were silenced, accepting that this life was the life you had to live when that was not the case. You can change your life at any time and at any age.

If you look at Ebenezer Scrooge in A Christmas Carol, he changed his life at an older age and was happier because of it. You couldn't see the signs that you needed to change your life because you had gotten too comfortable undertaking something that wasn't meant for you.

In the song, "Jingle Bells," the family ventures out on a sleigh ride, but they eventually come home. Even though you moved to another state, you've yet to find your home. That was the thing that worried me the most about you, Belle. While you're a strong and independent woman, you don't have a home. I don't mean home in the manner of a physical structure. I mean home in the soul of another human being. While you have moved mountains all by yourself, life is more beautiful when you find the right person to share it with.

That's why I took it upon myself to do a bit of matchmaking, which I hope you'll forgive me for. Selfishly, I had you go on this scavenger hunt because I knew you would need the help of my grandson. Since he was a little boy, Jake has always loved mysteries and puzzles. I knew he wouldn't be able to resist trying to figure out what tricks I had up my sleeve.

Jake is a wonderful young man, but he allowed his heart to grow cold after his broken engagement. You, Belle, have allowed your heart to grow cold as well by giving up your painting, and throwing yourself into your work. I secretly hoped that putting you two together on a given task would in some way help you heal each other. Maybe it's an old man's foolish dream that you both would fall in love and be together. But time will tell.

I want to leave you with one last thought, Belle. Home is not a place. Home is whatever makes your soul happy, whether it be a person, a hobby, a place, etc. Don't continue to let yourself be silent like a bell without a clapper. Stand up and allow yourself to ring loudly for the world to see. You are so much more than you give yourself credit for.

Take care of yourself and allow your heart to remain open so love will find its way inside.

-Sam

Belle continued to stare at the words long after she finished reading them. A tear formed in the corner of her eye and streamed down her cheek. Sam was right. Silence was no longer an option. Her life was a stagnant pool that demanded a change. She was destined for a greater stage. Rising to her feet, Belle grabbed her coat off the chair and put it on. As she headed downstairs, she dialed the number for the Chenello Museum. It was time to do things differently.

CHAPTER 34

Moonlight painted silver patterns on the wooden floor of Belle's bedroom. Opening the closet doors and drawers, she frantically searched for her purse. It was December Twenty-Third, the evening of the Christmas Gala. A thrill of anticipation coursed through her veins as she imagined the town's reaction to the transformed manor. Yet, a knot of anxiety twisted in her stomach at the thought of seeing Jake. Their last interaction had not been one of their finest moments.

"Belle, where are you?" Josie's face appeared on the screen of Belle's phone. She squinted her eyes. "What are you doing? You're fifteen minutes late. Everyone is arriving."

"Found it." Belle held up her purse in triumph as she emerged from under her bed. "I know. I know. I ran late signing the paperwork for the space. I wanted to get everything buttoned up today so I can hit the ground running in the new year." She took her sparkly emerald heels out of the closet and slipped her feet into them.

"You look stunning," gushed Josie. "I'm so proud of you, Belle. You have come a long way."

"Belle. What's taking so long?" Grayson's face appeared on the screen next to Josie. He whistled. "You look great, sis."

"Grayson, were you able to sneak it into the manor?" Belle put on her dangling earrings.

"Yes, I was. There were so many people coming in and out of Frost Manor all day that Jake never suspected a thing. I can't believe how many people have turned out for this event. The whole town must be here," exclaimed Grayson.

"Thank you. I'll be there in ten minutes. I'm leaving the house now," Belle replied.

"One last thing, sis. I don't know if this means anything, but I've noticed Jake glancing at the door every few minutes since the party started. It's as if he's waiting for someone." Grayson smirked.

Belle's heart fluttered in her chest. Maybe Jake missed her just as much as she missed him. "I'll see you in a few minutes." She ended the facetime and placed her phone into her green clutch, stopping in front of the mirror to give herself one final look.

The woman staring back at her was a stranger to the shattered soul who'd arrived in Falls Village just three weeks ago. Gone was the workaholic who'd traded life for promotions. The artist in her was back and a newfound joy radiated from her reflection. Belle liked this unfamiliar sensation that coursed through her veins.

Sam's words had been the wake-up call she needed. She would no longer be a silent bell. She would demand a life worthy of her. The gallery layoff had been the cruel twist of fate she needed to find her true place in the world.

Belle's fingers traced the lush green velvet of her mermaid gown. The straps hung off her shoulders, showcasing her muscular frame. Her long hair was accented with glittering combs. A diamond necklace accentuated her collarbone, while pear-shaped emerald earrings and a constellation of bracelets completed her glamorous ensemble.

Pausing, Belle remembered Sam's parting wisdom about keeping an open heart. Life blooms beautifully with the right person. She knew who the right person was. Fear gnawed at her and she hoped she hadn't ruined things beyond repair.

Covered in a faux fur shawl, Belle rushed to her car. This

time she was ready. There would be no hesitation and no distractions. She would tell Jake how she felt regardless of his response.

Miraculously, she found a parking spot at Frost Manor. The overwhelming turnout had surpassed her wildest expectations and she was beyond delighted.

Sam would have been so proud to see this.

Locking her car door, Belle hurried across the driveway, filled with an exhilaration she couldn't contain. Josie and Grayson waited for her by the front door.

"You made it." Josie gave her a hug. "You look beautiful."

Belle stepped back and admired her sister's elegant crimson gown and her brother's sophisticated black tuxedo. "You both look stunning." She glanced around. A chuckle escaped her lips as she remembered this had been where her first interaction with Jake had taken place. "Where is Jake?"

"Last I checked, he was in the ballroom. But I'm not sure where he went," replied Grayson.

"We know you want to talk to Jake, but first you need to see all your hard work." Josie grabbed Belle's hand and led her through the manor to the ballroom.

Belle stepped through the entrance that was framed by poinsettia-adorned pines. Her eyes widened as she saw the town had turned out in full support of the Frost family. The elegant attire of the residents was a shimmering tapestry against the winter night. Happiness lined the faces of the people of Falls Village, and filled Belle with pure joy. The delicious scent of Italian food wafted through the room. Glistening Christmas trees cast a magical glow about the space. A fire crackled in the hearth, and the melody of a string quartet created a warm ambiance. Guests mingled and placed their bids for the silent auction items.

Josie grabbed Belle's arm and pulled her closer. "You should hear everyone raving about Jake. They all speak highly of him now. No one sees him as a beast anymore."

Belle was relieved to hear that.

Grayson appeared at her side. "I overheard a few people talking. The man you're looking for is in the solarium. Go to him."

Belle hugged her siblings. "You're the best. Thank you."

Clutching her gown, Belle left the ballroom and hurried down the hall toward the solarium. Wrapping her fingers around the handles, the doors yielded to her touch, revealing the haven fragrant with rose blossoms. Jake stood silhouetted against the large glass windows. He gazed out into the wintry landscape. His hands were in his pockets, and Belle couldn't help but admire how nicely his tuxedo accentuated his muscular frame.

The doors clicked shut and Belle stepped into the room. Her heart pounded in her chest. With a steady breath, she pushed away the doubts that advised her to turn back. *No second-guessing this time. Go for it.*

"Jake," Belle breathed, her voice barely a whisper.

Jake spun around, his eyes locking onto hers as disbelief crossed his face. A radiant smile spread across his lips as if the sun had just burst through a cloudy sky.

"Belle. I didn't think you would come back." His voice trembled slightly, and his eyes held a mixture of relief and longing. He stepped toward her, his arms outstretched.

"I never wanted to leave." Before doubts could paralyze her, Belle ran across the room into Jake's arms. Taking his face in her hands, she kissed him. His arms tightened around her waist as her fingers tangled in his hair. They claimed each other's lips in a desperate, hungry plea. Jake's kiss ignited a wildfire within her and confirmed what her heart had always known. Jake was her home. Love was a gamble, but the prize was everything. A serene calmness washed over Belle as happiness stirred in her soul. In the moonlight embrace of the solarium, she had found her sanctuary.

"I'm sorry, Jake," Belle said as she pulled away from his lips. "I shouldn't have gone into your garbage and taken the photo. I never meant to hurt you."

Jake kissed her again. "Don't apologize. I'm the one who needs to apologize. I allowed my pain to mold me into a person that I'm not proud of, but I realize now that Madison did me a favor. I'm glad the wish I made on the Wishing Bell didn't come true. It brought me to the person I was truly meant to be with. You." He brushed a piece of hair behind Belle's ear. "Belle Winters, when you appeared on my doorstep demanding to know why the manor wasn't decorated, I didn't realize it at the time, but you were the best thing that ever happened to me." He pulled her closer to him and rested his cheek on the top of her head. "I read Grandpa's letter."

"I read mine, too."

"Grandpa said I've allowed heartbreak to become my world. My pain has made me miss out on one of life's greatest gifts: love. He admitted he's been a secret matchmaker and we would be perfect for each other. Turns out he was right. Now I see why he wanted you to have this necklace." Jake reached into his pocket and pulled out the heart-shaped piece of jewelry. "The engraving on the back matches the quote on the sign from the cabin. Home is not a place. Home is a person. Many years ago, my grandpa made this pendant for my grandma because she was his home. You're my home, Belle. You're the one I want to be with. I know you're going back to New York City, but I don't want to lose you. I want to make this work." He gently fastened the necklace around Belle's neck. The pendant rested delicately on her chest, layered among the other pieces of jewelry.

"I'm not going back to New York City," Belle revealed as she grabbed his hands. "I turned down the job. You were right. One rejection shouldn't have ended my love of painting. I'm going to open an art gallery here in Falls Village. I want to spotlight indie artists and offer art classes for anyone who wants to learn. This is my new path."

Jake kissed her. "I'm proud of you, Belle."

"That has been my project for the past few days. A vacancy opened downtown; it's right near my sister's bakery. I signed the lease this afternoon. Two of my friends from the city are going to invest in the art gallery. We're going to start the remodel after Christmas. I hired a realtor and will be looking for a house of my own, too."

Jake hugged her. "That's wonderful news. But I have another confession to make. I took pictures of the painting you created of Frost Manor, and I sent them to a contact at the Silver Hollow Art Gallery in Montpelier." Reaching into the inside pocket of his suit, he handed Belle a letter. "They want to feature your work in their upcoming exhibit."

Belle's heart soared and she hugged him tight. "Thank you, Jake. Thank you." Her gaze fell to the coffee table. To her surprise, the dreadful black rose was gone. In its place radiated a ruby blossom.

"What happened to the black rose?" asked Belle.

A smile crept across Jake's face. "It's gone for good. My heart is no longer broken. It's healed thanks to you, Belle. Now the red rose sits in its place to symbolize true love and happiness."

Soft strains of instrumental music seeped through the solarium doors, creating a dreamy ambiance around them. Belle remembered there was a ballroom full of guests down the hall.

"We should get back to the gala." Jake held out his hand to her.

"Yes, but first, I have a surprise for you." Belle intertwined her fingers with his.

Hand in hand, they returned to the ballroom where the residents of Falls Village were glowing in the festive atmosphere.

Belle led Jake over to the fireplace that was decorated with poinsettias. A covered portrait stood in front of the stone structure.

"What's this?" Jake looked over at Belle who smiled.

"Look underneath," she replied.

Jake lifted the sheet to reveal a painting of Sam and Agnes Frost at the Christmas Gala long ago. Their arms were intertwined, and the couple looked into each other's eyes, smiling and laughing.

"It looks just like the photo from the fireplace." Jake turned to Belle. "You painted that?"

Belle nodded. "You inspired me to get back into painting. It's my gift to you. Since we're celebrating the Frost family, it's only right their presence is at the ball, too."

Jake kissed her forehead. "Since we're giving each other gifts, I have a surprise for you." Taking her arm, he led her out of the ballroom to the adjacent room. The door stood open, revealing a line of expectant people. A ringing pierced the air, drawing Belle's attention.

As she stepped inside, Belle remembered this space had been empty a few weeks ago. Now it was decorated with Christmas trees, garland, and twinkling lights. In the center, on a red rug, stood the Wishing Bell. The clapper had been reattached, and people of all ages took their turn approaching the masterpiece and making a wish.

"You fixed it." Belle squeezed Jake's arm.

Jake nodded. "I realized that my grandpa's mission was to spread joy and happiness throughout the state, and I want to do the same. Everyone deserves to have a special wish at Christmas."

A radiant smile broke across Belle's face.

"Let's leave the guests to their wishes," Jake whispered in her ear as the melody from the string quartet floated into the room. "May I have this dance?"

Belle nodded, allowing Jake to lead her back to the ballroom and onto the dance floor with the other couples. As they swayed to the music, her gaze drifted to the opposite side of the room. A Santa Claus station had been set up, and a line of children eagerly awaited their opportunity to tell Santa their last-minute desires. A plump, jolly man sat on the throne with a white beard, spectacles, and a red suit. Their eyes met across the room, and he gave her a wink. Belle's eyes widened as she realized it was Pasquale Fontana.

Jake's arms tightened around her waist as she rested her hands on his shoulders. Together, they watched the happy people celebrating the magic of the holiday.

"In the end, the Beast did find his Beauty after all," Jake murmured in her ear. "And she's more beautiful than any fairytale."

Belle leaned in and kissed him softly. "Yes, he did."

Hickory Dickory Death

A Soul for a Soul

I am a woman

I am a man

I am the one who seeks revenge

In Victorian Era England, five people come face to face with life's most fear entity: Death

The Sapphora Series

Book 1: Shards of Secrecy

Egyptian Mythology meets modern day adventure in a spellbinding quest filled with sorcery and forbidden romance.

ACKNOWLEDGMENTS

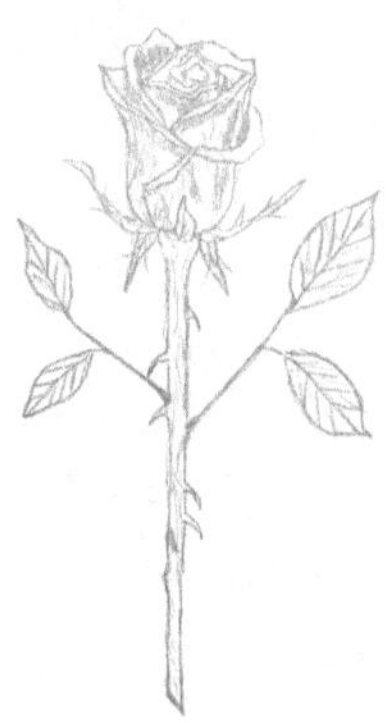

Publishing a book is no joke, and it wouldn't be possible without the amazing people who have supported me.

My biggest thank you goes to my sister, Ashley, who has been my partner in crime from day one. Without you, this book wouldn't have been possible. Thank you for being the person I can bounce ideas around with, reading my story when it was in the raw version, and editing for me when I kept scrapping my story over and over. Also, your beautiful drawings have made this book unique and special. I love doing this author journey with you.

Mom and Dad, thank you for your support and for always being here for me. No matter what, you always made the holidays special for Ashley and I. I appreciate you both.

Edith, you have been with me on this author journey from my first publication until now. Thank you for always being here for me.

To my amazing friends: Stephanie Tramontanois, Eloise Waterbury, Corinthian Hughes, and Eva Schultz, thank you for always being here to listen, laugh, and cheer me on. I'm grateful for your friendship.

Thank you to my beautiful author friends who I adore: Jennifer Kropf, Ashley Steffenson, Bekah Berge, Alice Ivinya, Roxie Cohen, Lyndsey Hall, and Magaidh Dunbroch. You all inspire me and motivate me every day to improve as a writer. I am so proud of how far all of you have come and how you continue to chase your dreams.

Thank you to my cover designer Emily. As always, your covers exceed my expectations. Thank you for taking my ideas and making them into beautiful art. You are so talented.

Thank you to my editor Melissa Cole. I appreciate you helping make my manuscript into the best version it can be.

Thank you to my formatter, Magaidh Dunbroch. I'm so happy to do this author journey with you.

Thank you to my beta readers: Jess Fuller, Trivina Zimmerman, Amber Kirsten, Saydee Black, Dejah Bonilla, Heather Douglass, Casie Ohara, Alicia Ramos, Ashley Thorp, Jennifer Christensen, Jessica Botteri, Bretnie Shepherd, and Marcia Albright. Thank you for reading my story when it was in its early stage and giving me feedback.

Lastly, thank you reader for reading my book. Out of all the books in the world, you have chosen mine to read and that means the world to me. I am forever grateful for your support. Thank you for believing in me and helping make my dreams come true.

I hope the magic of the holiday season brings you closer to the ones you love, and fills your soul with happiness.

ABOUT THE AUTHOR

N.D. Testa realized at a young age that her true passion is telling stories. An Italian-American author who lives in the United States, her goal is to give readers an escape from reality with her books. When she doesn't have a pen in her hand, she can be found at the gym. A fashionista and skincare addict, N.D. Testa also enjoys snowboarding, riding horses, and learning new languages. In addition to being an animal lover, she dreams of traveling the world. At night she enjoys being by the fire with a cup of tea in her hands.